The Manxman
Part I

by

Sir Hall Caine

ABOUT THE AUTHOR

Sir Thomas Henry Hall, better known as Hall Caine, was a British novelist, dramatist, short story writer, poet, and critic in the late nineteenth and early twentieth centuries. Caine enjoyed exceptional fame throughout his lifetime. He published fifteen novels on infidelity, divorce, domestic abuse, illegitimacy, infanticide, religious prejudice, and women's rights, becoming a worldwide literary celebrity and selling 10 million copies. Caine was the highest-paid novelist of his day. The Eternal City is the first novel to sell more than one million copies globally. Caine was born in Runcorn to a Manx father and a Cumbrian mother, but grew up in Liverpool. Caine received architectural draughtsman training after completing four years in school. He spent his boyhood holidays with family in the Isle of Man. At the age of seventeen, he spent a year as a schoolmaster in Maughold. After that, he returned to Liverpool and began a career in journalism, eventually becoming a leader writer for the Liverpool Mercury. As a lecturer and theatre critic, he formed a network of prominent literary contacts who impacted him. Caine traveled to London at Dante Gabriel Rossetti's recommendation and stayed with the poet, serving as secretary and companion throughout Rossetti's final years.

CONTENTS

PART I
BOYS TOGETHER

I

Old Deemster Christian of Ballawhaine was a hard man—hard on the outside, at all events. They called him Iron Christian, and people said, "Don't turn that iron hand against you." Yet his character was stamped with nobleness as well as strength. He was not a man of icy nature, but he loved to gather icicles about him. There was fire enough underneath, at which he warmed his old heart when alone, but he liked the air to be congealed about his face. He was a man of a closed soul. One had to wrench open the dark chamber where he kept his feelings; but the man who had done that had uncovered his nakedness, and he cut him off for ever. That was how it happened with his son, the father of Philip.

He had two sons; the elder was an impetuous creature, a fiery spirit, one of the masterful souls who want the restraint of the curb if they are not to hurry headlong into the abyss. Old Deemster Christian had called this boy Thomas Wilson, after the serene saint who had once been Bishop of Man. He was intended, however, for the law, not for the Church. The office of Deemster never has been and never can be hereditary; yet the Christians of Ballawhaine had been Deemsters through six generations, and old Iron Christian expected that Thomas Wilson Christian would succeed him. But there was enough uncertainty about the succession to make merit of more value than precedent in the selection, and so the old man had brought up his son to the English bar, and afterwards called him to practise in the Manx one. The young fellow had not altogether rewarded his father's endeavours. During his residence in England, he had acquired certain modern doctrines which were highly obnoxious to the old Deemster. New views on property, new ideas about woman and marriage, new theories concerning religion (always re-christened superstition), the usual barnacles of young vessels fresh from unknown waters; but the old man was no shipwright in harbour who has learnt the art of removing them without injury to the hull. The

Deemster knew these notions when he met with them in the English newspapers. There was something awesome in their effect on his stay-at-home imagination, as of vices confusing and difficult to true men that walk steadily; but, above all, very far off, over the mountains and across the sea, like distant cities of Sodom, only waiting for Sodom's doom. And yet, lo! here they were in a twinkling, shunted and shot into his own house and his own stackyard.

"I suppose now," he said, with a knowing look, "you think Jack as good as his master?"

"No, sir," said his son gravely; "generally much better."

Iron Christian altered his will. To his elder son he left only a life-interest in Ballawhaine. "That boy will be doing something," he said, and thus he guarded against consequences. He could not help it; he was ashamed, but he could not conquer his shame—the fiery old man began to nurse a grievance against his son.

The two sons of the Deemster were like the inside and outside of a bowl, and that bowl was the Deemster himself. If Thomas Wilson the elder had his father's inside fire and softness, Peter, the younger, had his father's outside ice and iron. Peter was little and almost misshapen, with a pair of shoulders that seemed to be trying to meet over a hollow chest and limbs that splayed away into vacancy. And if Nature had been grudging with him, his father was not more kind. He had been brought up to no profession, and his expectations were limited to a yearly charge out of his brother's property. His talk was bitter, his voice cold, he laughed little, and had never been known to cry. He had many things against him.

Besides these sons, Deemster Christian had a girl in his household, but to his own consciousness the fact was only a kind of peradventure. She was his niece, the child of his only brother, who had died in early manhood. Her name was Ann Charlotte de la Tremouille, called after the lady of Rushen, for the family of Christian had their share of the heroic that is in all men. She had fine eyes, a weak mouth, and great timidity. Gentle airs floated always about her, and a sort of nervous brightness twinkled over her, as of a glen with the sun flickering through. Her mother died when she was a child of twelve, and in the house of her uncle and her cousins she had been brought up among men and boys.

One day Peter drew the Deemster aside and told him (with expressions of shame, interlarded with praises of his own acuteness) a story of his brother. It was about a girl. Her name was Mona Crellin; she lived on the hill at Ballure House, half a mile south of Ramsey, and was daughter of a man called Billy Ballure, a retired sea-captain, and hail-fellow-well-met with all the jovial spirits of the town.

There was much noise and outcry, and old Iron sent for his son.

"What's this I hear?" he cried, looking him down. "A woman? So that's what your fine learning comes to, eh? Take care, sir! take care! No son of mine shall disgrace himself. The day he does that he will be put to the door."

Thomas held himself in with a great effort.

"Disgrace?" he said. "What disgrace, sir, if you please?"

"What disgrace, sir?" repeated the Deemster, mocking his son in a mincing treble. Then he roared, "Behaving dishonourably to a poor girl— that what's disgrace, sir! Isn't it enough? eh? eh?"

"More than enough," said the young man. "But who is doing it? I'm not."

"Then you're doing worse. *Did* I say worse? Of course I said worse. Worse, sir, worse! Do you hear me? Worse! You are trapsing around Ballure, and letting that poor girl take notions. I'll have no more of it. Is this what I sent you to England for? Aren't you ashamed of yourself? Keep your place, sir; keep your place. A poor girl's a poor girl, and a Deemster's a Deemster."

"Yes, sir," said Thomas, suddenly firing up, "and a man's a man. As for the shame, I need be ashamed of nothing that is not shameful; and the best proof I can give you that I mean no dishonour by the girl is that I intend to marry her."

"What? You intend to—what? Did I hear——"

The old Deemster turned his good ear towards his son's face, and the young man repeated his threat. Never fear! No poor girl should be misled by him. He was above all foolish conventions.

Old Iron Christian was dumbfounded. He gasped, he stared, he stammered, and then fell on his son with hot reproaches.

"What? Your wife? Wife? That trollop!—that minx! that—and daughter of that sot, too, that old rip, that rowdy blatherskite—that——And my own son is to lift his hand to cut his throat! Yes, sir, cut his throat——And I am to stand by! No, no! I say no, sir, no!"

The young man made some further protest, but it was lost in his father's clamour.

"You will, though? You will? Then your hat is your house, sir. Take to it—take to it!"

"No need to tell me twice, father."

"Away then—away to your woman—your jade! God, keep my hands off him!"

The old man lifted his clenched fist, but his son had flung out of the room. It was not the Deemster only who feared he might lay hands on his own flesh and blood.

"Stop! come back, you dog! Listen! I've not done yet. Stop! you hotheaded rascal, stop! Can't you hear a man out then? Come back! Thomas Wilson, come back, sir! Thomas! Thomas! Tom! Where is he? Where's the boy?"

Old Iron Christian had made after his son bareheaded down to the road, shouting his name in a broken roar, but the young man was gone. Then he went back slowly, his grey hair playing in the wind. He was all iron outside, but all father within.

That day the Deemster altered his will a second time, and his elder son was disinherited.

II

Peter succeeded in due course to the estate of Ballawhaine, but he was not a lawyer, and the line of the Deemsters Christian was broken.

Meantime Thomas Wilson Christian had been married to Mona Crellin without delay. He loved her, but he had been afraid of her ignorance, afraid also (notwithstanding his principles) of the difference in their social rank, and had half intended to give her up when his father's reproaches had come to fire his anger and to spur his courage. As soon as she became his wife he realised the price he had paid for her. Happiness could not come of such a beginning. He had broken every tie in making the one which brought him down. The rich disowned him, and the poor lost respect for him.

"It's positively indecent," said one. "It's potatoes marrying herrings," said another. It was little better than hunger marrying thirst.

In the general downfall of his fame his profession failed him. He lost heart and ambition. His philosophy did not stand him in good stead, for it had no value in the market to which he brought it. Thus, day by day, he sank deeper into the ooze of a wrecked and wasted life.

The wife did not turn out well. She was a fretful person, with a good face, a bad shape, a vacant mind, and a great deal of vanity. She had liked her husband a little as a lover, but when she saw that her marriage brought her nobody's envy, she fell into a long fit of the vapours. Eventually she made herself believe that she was an ill-used person. She never ceased to complain of her fate. Everybody treated her as if she had laid plans for her husband's ruin.

The husband continued to love her, but little by little he grew to despise her also. When he made his first plunge, he had prided himself on indulging an heroic impulse. He was not going to deliver a good woman to dishonour because she seemed to be an obstacle to his success. But she had never realised his sacrifice. She did not appear to understand that he might have been a great man in the island, but that love and honour had held him back. Her ignorance was pitiful, and he was ashamed of it. In earning the contempt of others he had not saved himself from self-contempt.

The old sailor died suddenly in a fit of drunkenness at a fair, and husband and wife came into possession of his house and property at Ballure. This did not improve the relations between them. The woman perceived that their positions were reversed. She was the bread-bringer now. One day, at a slight that her husband's people had put upon her in the street, she reminded him, in order to re-establish her wounded vanity, that but for her and hers he would not have so much as a roof to cover him.

Yet the man continued to love her in spite of all. And she was not at first a degraded being. At times she was bright and cheerful, and, except in the worst spells of her vapours, she was a brisk and busy woman. The house was sweet and homely. There was only one thing to drive him away from it, but that was the greatest thing of all. Nevertheless they had their cheerful hours together.

A child was born, a boy, and they called him Philip. He was the beginning of the end between them; the iron stay that held them together and yet apart. The father remembered his misfortunes in the presence of his son, and the mother was stung afresh by the recollection of disappointed hopes. The boy was the true heir of Ballawhaine, but the inheritance was lost to him by his father's fault and he had nothing.

Philip grew to be a winsome lad. There was something sweet and amiable and big-hearted, and even almost great, in him. One day the father sat in the garden by the mighty fuchsia-tree that grows on the lawn, watching his little fair-haired son play at marbles on the path with two big lads whom he had enticed out of the road, and another more familiar playmate—the little barefooted boy Peter, from the cottage by the water-trough. At first Philip lost, and with grunts of satisfaction the big ones promptly pocketed their gains. Then Philip won, and little curly Peter was stripped naked, and his lip began to fall. At that Philip paused, held his head aside, and considered, and then said quite briskly, "Peter hadn't a fair chance that time—here, let's give him another go."

The father's throat swelled, and he went indoors to the mother and said, "I think—perhaps I'm to blame—but somehow I think our boy isn't like other boys. What do you say? Foolish? May be so, may be so! No difference? Well, no—no!"

But deep down in the secret place of his heart, Thomas Wilson Christian, broken man, uprooted tree, wrecked craft in the mud and slime, began to cherish a fond idea. The son would regain all that his father had lost! He had gifts, and he should be brought up to the law; a large nature, and he should be helped to develop it; a fine face which all must love, a sense of justice, and a great wealth of the power of radiating happiness. Deemster?

Why not? Ballawhaine? Who could tell? The biggest, noblest, greatest of all Manxmen! God knows!

Only—only he must be taught to fly from his father's dangers. Love? Then let him love where he can also respect—but never outside his own sphere. The island was too little for that. To love and to despise was to suffer the torments of the damned.

Nourishing these dreams, the poor man began to be tortured by every caress the mother gave her son, and irritated by every word she spoke to him. Her grammar was good enough for himself, and the exuberant caresses of her maudlin moods were even sometimes pleasant, but the boy must be degraded by neither.

The woman did not reach to these high thoughts, but she was not slow to interpret the casual byplay in which they found expression. Her husband was taiching her son to dis-respeck her. She wouldn't have thought it of him—she wouldn't really. But it was always the way when a plain practical woman married on the quality. Imperence and dis-respeck—that's the capers! Imperence and disrespeck from the ones that's doing nothing and beholden to you for everything. It was shocking! It was disthressing!

In such outbursts would her jealousy taunt him with his poverty, revile him for his idleness, and square accounts with him for the manifest preference of the boy. He could bear them with patience when they were alone, but in Philip's presence they were as gall and wormwood, and whips and scorpions.

"Go, my lad, go," he would sometimes whimper, and hustle the boy out of the way.

"No," the woman would cry, "stop and see the man your father is."

And the father would mutter, "He might see the woman his mother is as well."

But when she had pinned them together, and the boy had to hear her out, the man would drop his forehead on the table and break into groans and tears. Then the woman would change quite suddenly, and put her arms about him and kiss him and weep over him. He could defend himself from neither her insults nor her embraces. In spite of everything he loved her. That was where the bitterness of the evil lay. But for the love he bore her, he might have got her off his back and been his own man once more. He would make peace with her and kiss her again, and they would both kiss the boy, and be tender, and even cheerful.

Philip was still a child, but he saw the relations of his parents, and in his own way he understood everything. He loved his father best, but he did not hate his mother. She was nearly always affectionate, though often jealous of the father's greater love and care for him, and sometimes irritable from that cause alone. But the frequent broils between them were like blows that left scars on his body. He slept in a cot in the same room, and he would cover up his head in the bedclothes at night with a feeling of fear and physical pain.

A man cannot fight against himself for long. That deadly enemy is certain to slay. When Philip was six years old his father lay sick of his last sickness. The wife had fallen into habits of intemperance by this time, and stage by stage she had descended to the condition of an utterly degraded woman. There was something to excuse her. She had been disappointed in the great stakes of life; she had earned disgrace where she had looked for admiration. She was vain, and could not bear misfortune; and she had no deep well of love from which to drink when the fount of her pride ran dry. If her husband had indulged her with a little pity, everything might have gone along more easily. But he had only loved her and been ashamed. And now that he lay near to his death, the love began to ebb and the shame to deepen into dread.

He slept little at night, and as often as he closed his eyes certain voices of mocking and reproach seemed to be constantly humming in his ears.

"Your son!" they would cry. "What is to become of him? Your dreams! Your great dreams! Deemster! Ballawhaine! God knows what! You are leaving the boy; who is to bring him up? His mother? Think of it!"

At last a ray of pale sunshine broke on the sleepless wrestler with the night, and he became almost happy. "I'll speak to the boy," he thought. "I will tell him my own history, concealing nothing. Yes, I will tell him of my own father also, God rest him, the stern old man—severe, yet just."

An opportunity soon befell. It was late at night—very late. The woman was sleeping off a bout of intemperance somewhere below; and the boy, with the innocence and ignorance of his years in all that the solemn time foreboded, was bustling about the room with mighty eagerness, because he knew that he ought to be in bed.

"I'm staying up to intend on you, father," said the boy.

The father answered with a sigh.

"Don't you asturb yourself, father. I'll intend on you."

The father's sigh deepened to a moan.

"If you want anything 'aticular, just call me; d'ye see, father?"

And away went the boy like a gleam of light. Presently he came back, leaping like the dawn. He was carrying, insecurely, a jug of poppy-head and camomile, which had been prescribed as a lotion.

"Poppy heads, father! Poppy-heads is good, I can tell ye."

"Why arn't you in bed, child?" said the father. "You must be tired."

"No, I'm not tired, father. I was just feeling a bit of tired, and then I took a smell of poppy-heads and away went the tiredness to Jericho. They *is* good."

The little white head was glinting off again when the father called it back.

"Come here, my boy." The child went up to the bedside, and the father ran his fingers lovingly through the long fair hair.

"Do you think, Philip, that twenty, thirty, forty years hence, when you are a man—aye, a big man, little one—do you think you will remember what I shall say to you now?"

"Why, yes, father, if it's anything 'aticular, and if it isn't you can amind me of it, can't you, father?"

The father shook his head. "I shall not be here then, my boy. I am going away——"

"Going away, father? May I come too?"

"Ah! I wish you could, little one. Yes, truly I almost wish you could."

"Then you'll let me go with you, father! Oh, I *am* glad, father." And the boy began to caper and dance, to go down on all fours, and leap about the floor like a frog.

The father fell back on his pillow with a heaving breast. Vain! vain! What was the use of speaking? The child's outlook was life; his own was death; they had no common ground; they spoke different tongues. And, after all, how could he suffer the sweet innocence of the child's soul to look down into the stained and scarred chamber of his ruined heart?

"You don't understand me, Philip. I mean that I am going—to die. Yes, darling, and, only that I am leaving you behind, I should be glad to go. My life has been wasted, Philip. In the time to come, when men speak of your father, you will be ashamed. Perhaps you will not remember then that whatever he was he was a good father to you, for at least he loved you dearly. Well, I must needs bow to the will of God, but if I could only hope that you would live to restore my name when I am gone.... Philip, are you— don't cry, my darling. There, there, kiss me. We'll say no more about it then.

Perhaps it's not true, although father tolded you? Well, perhaps not. And now undress and slip into bed before mother comes. See, there's your night-dress at the foot of the crib. Wants some buttons, does it? Never mind—in with you—that's a boy."

Impossible, impossible! And perhaps unnecessary. Who should say? Young as the child was, he might never forget what he had seen and heard. Some day it must have its meaning for him. Thus the father comforted himself. Those jangling quarrels which had often scorched his brain like iron—the memory of their abject scenes came to him then, with a sort of bleeding solace!

Meanwhile, with little catching sobs, which he struggled to repress, the boy lay down in his crib. When half-way gone towards the mists of the land of sleep, he started up suddenly, and called "Good night, father," and his father answered him "Good night."

Towards three o'clock the next morning there was great commotion in the house. The servant was scurrying up and downstairs, and the mistress, wringing her hands, was tramping to and fro in the sick-room, crying in a tone of astonishment, as if the thought had stolen upon her unawares, "Why, he's going! How didn't somebody tell me before?"

The eyes of the sinking man were on the crib. "Philip," he faltered. They lifted the boy out of his bed, and brought him in his night-dress to his father's side; and the father twisted about and took him into his arms, still half asleep and yawning. Then the mother, recovering from the stupidity of her surprise, broke into paroxysms of weeping, and fell over her husband's breast and kissed and kissed him.

For once her kisses had no response. The man was dying miserably, for he was thinking of her and of the boy. Sometimes he babbled over Philip in a soft, inarticulate gurgle; sometimes he looked up at his wife's face with a stony stare, and then he clung the closer to the boy, as if he would never let him go. The dark hour came, and still he held the boy in his arms. They had to release the child at last from his father's dying grip.

The dead of the night was gone by this time, and the day was at the point of dawn; the sparrows in the eaves were twittering, and the tide, which was at its lowest ebb, was heaving on the sand far out in the bay with the sound as of a rookery awakening. Philip remembered afterwards that his mother cried so much that he was afraid, and that when he had been dressed she took him downstairs, where they all ate breakfast together, with the sun shining through the blinds.

The mother did not live to overshadow her son's life. Sinking yet lower in habits of intemperance, she stayed indoors from week-end to week-end, seated herself like a weeping willow by the fireside, and drank and drank. Her excesses led to delusions. She saw ghosts perpetually. To avoid such of them as haunted the death-room of her husband, she had a bed made up on a couch in the parlour, and one morning she was found face downwards stretched out beside it on the floor.

Then Philip's father's cousin, always called his Aunty Nan, came to Ballure House to bring him up. His father had been her favourite cousin, and, in spite of all that had happened, he had been her lifelong hero also. A deep and secret tenderness, too timid to be quite aware of itself, had been lying in ambush in her heart through all the years of his miserable life with Mona. At the death of the old Deemster, her other cousin, Peter, had married and cast her off. But she was always one of those woodland herbs which are said to give out their sweetest fragrance after they have been trodden on and crushed. Philip's father had been her hero, her lost one and her love, and Philip was his father's son.

III

Little curly Pete, with the broad, bare feet, the tousled black head, the jacket half way up his back like a waistcoat with sleeves, and the hole in his trousers where the tail of his shirt should have been, was Peter Quilliam, and he was the natural son of Peter Christian. In the days when that punctilious worthy set himself to observe the doings of his elder brother at Ballure, he found it convenient to make an outwork of the hedge in front of the thatched house that stood nearest. Two persons lived in the cottage, father and daughter—Tom Quilliam, usually called Black Tom, and Bridget Quilliam, getting the name of Bridget Black Tom.

The man was a short, gross creature, with an enormous head and a big, open mouth, showing broken teeth that were black with the juice of tobacco. The girl was by common judgment and report a gawk—a great, slow-eyed, comely-looking, comfortable, easy-going gawk. Black Tom was a thatcher, and with his hair poking its way through the holes in his straw hat, he tramped the island in pursuit of his calling. This kept him from home for days together, and in that fact Peter Christian, while shadowing the morality of his brother, found his own opportunity.

When the child was born, neither the thatcher nor his daughter attempted to father it. Peter Christian paid twenty pounds to the one and eighty to the other in Manx pound-notes, the boys daubed their door to show that the house was dishonoured, and that was the end of everything.

The girl went through her "censures" silently, or with only one comment. She had borrowed the sheet in which she appeared in church from Miss Christian of Ballawhaine, and when she took it back, the good soul of the sweet lady thought to improve the occasion.

"I was wondering, Bridget," she said gravely, "what you were thinking of when you stood with Bella and Liza before the congregation last Sunday morning"—two other Magda-lenes had done penance by Bridget's side.

"'Deed, mistress," said the girl, "I was thinkin' there wasn't a sheet at one of them to match mine for whiteness. I'd 'a been ashamed to be seen in the like of theirs."

Bridget may have been a gawk, but she did two things which were not gawkish. Putting the eighty greasy notes into the foot of an old stocking, she sewed them up in the ticking of her bed, and then christened her baby Peter. The money was for the child if she should not live to rear him, and the name was her way of saying that a man's son was his son in spite of law or devil.

After that she kept both herself and her child by day labour in the fields, weeding and sowing potatoes, and following at the tail of the reapers, for sixpence a day dry days, and fourpence all weathers. She might have badgered the heir of Ballawhaine, but she never did so. That person came into his inheritance, got himself elected member for Ramsey in the House of Keys, married Nessy Taubman, daughter of the rich brewer, and became the father of another son. Such were the doings in the big house down in the valley, while up in the thatched cottage behind the water-trough, on potatoes and herrings and barley bonnag, lived Bridget and her little Pete.

Pete's earliest recollections were of a boy who lived at the beautiful white house with the big fuchsia, by the turn of the road over the bridge that crossed the glen. This was Philip Christian, half a year older than himself, although several inches shorter, with long yellow hair and rosy cheeks, and dressed in a velvet suit of knickerbockers. Pete worshipped him in his simple way, hung about him, fetched and carried for him, and looked up to him as a marvel of wisdom and goodness and pluck.

His first memory of Philip was of sleeping with him, snuggled up by his side in the dark, hushed and still in a narrow bed with iron ends to it, and of leaping up in the morning and laughing. Philip's father—a tall, white gentleman, who never laughed at all, and only smiled sometimes— had found him in the road in the evening waiting for his mother to come home from the fields, that he might light the fire in the cottage, and running about in the meantime to keep himself warm, and not too hungry.

His second memory was of Philip guiding him round the drawing-room (over thick carpets, on which his bare feet made no noise), and showing him the pictures on the walls, and telling him what they meant. One (an engraving of St. John, with a death's-head and a crucifix) was, according to this grim and veracious guide, a picture of a brigand who killed his victims, and always skinned their skulls with a cross-handled dagger. After that his memories of Philip and himself were as two gleams of sunshine which mingle and become one.

Philip was a great reader of noble histories. He found them, frayed and tattered, at the bottom of a trunk that had tin corners and two padlocks, and stood in the room looking towards the harbour where his mother's father, the old sailor, had slept. One of them was his special favourite, and he used to read it aloud to Pete. It told of the doings of the Carrasdhoo men. They were a bold band of desperadoes, the terror of all the island. Sometimes they worked in the fields at ploughing, and reaping, and stacking, the same as common practical men; and sometimes they lived in houses, just like the house by the water-trough. But when the wind was rising in the nor-nor-west, and there was a taste of the brine on your lips, they would be up, and say, "The sea's calling us—we must be going." Then they would live in rocky caves of the coast where nobody could reach them, and there would be fires lit at night in tar-barrels, and shouting, and singing, and carousing; and after that there would be ships' rudders, and figure heads, and masts coming up with the tide, and sometimes dead bodies on the beach of sailors they had drowned—only foreign ones though—hundreds and tons of them. But that was long ago, the Carrasdhoo men were dead, and the glory of their day was departed.

One quiet evening, after an awesome reading of this brave history, Philip, sitting on his haunches at the gable, with Pete like another white frog beside him, said quite suddenly, "Hush! What's that?"

"I wonder," said Pete.

There was never a sound in the air above the rustle of a leaf, and Pete's imagination could carry him no further.

"Pete," said Philip, with awful gravity, "the sea's calling me."

"And me," said Pete solemnly.

Early that night the two lads were down at the most desolate part of Port Mooar, in a cave under the scraggy black rocks of Gobny-Garvain, kindling a fire of gorse and turf inside the remains of a broken barrel.

"See that tremendous sharp rock below low water?" said Philip.

"Don't I, though?" said Pete.

There was never a rock the size of a currycomb between them and the line of the sky.

"That's what we call a reef," said Philip. "Wait a bit and you'll see the ships go splitting on top of it like—like——"

"Like a tay-pot," said Pete.

"We'll save the women, though," said Philip. "Shall we save the women, Pete? We always do."

"Aw, yes, the women—and the boys," said Pete thoughtfully.

Philip had his doubts about the boys, but he would not quarrel. It was nearly dark, and growing very cold. The lads croodled down by the crackling blaze, and tried to forget that they had forgotten tea-time.

"We never has to mind a bit of hungry," said Philip stoutly.

"Never a ha'p'orth," said Pete.

"Only when the job's done we have hams and flitches and things for supper."

"Aw, yes, ateing and drinking to the full."

"Rum, Pete, we always drinks rum."

"We has to," said Pete.

"None of your tea," said Philip.

"Coorse not, none of your ould grannie's two-penny tay," said Pete.

It was quite dark by this time, and the tide was rising rapidly. There was not a star in the sky, and not a light on the sea except the revolving light of the lightship far a Way. The boys crept closer together and began to think of home. Philip remembered Aunty Nan. When he had stolen away on hands and knees under the parlour window she had been sewing at his new check night-shirt. A night-shirt for a Carrasdhoo man had seemed to be ridiculous then; but where was Aunty Nannie now? Pete remembered his mother—she would be racing round the houses and crying; and he had visions of Black Tom—he would be racing round also and swearing.

"Shouldn't we sing something, Phil?" said Pete, with a gurgle in his throat.

"Sing!" said Philip, with as much scorn as he could summon, "and give them warning we're watching for them! Well, you *are* a pretty, Mr. Pete! But just you wait till the ships goes wrecking on the rocks—I mean the reefs— and the dead men's coming up like corks—hundreds and ninety and dozens of them; my jove! yes, then you'll hear me singing."

The darkness deepened, and the voice of the sea began to moan through the back of the cave, the gorse crackled no longer, and the turf burned in a dull red glow. Night with its awfulness had come down, and the boys were cut off from everything.

"They don't seem to be coming—not yet," said Philip, in a husky whisper.

"Maybe it's the same as fishing," said Pete; "sometimes you catch and sometimes you don't."

"That's it," said Philip eagerly, "generally you don't—and then you both haves to go home and come again," he added nervously.

But neither of the boys stirred. Outside the glow of the fire the blackness looked terrible. Pete nuzzled up to Philip's side, and, being untroubled by imaginative fears, soon began to feel drowsy. The sound of his measured breathing startled Philip with the terror of loneliness.

"Honour bright, Mr. Pete," he faltered, nudging the head on his shoulder, and trying to keep his voice from shaking; "*you* call yourself a second mate, and leaving all the work to me!"

The second mate was penitent, but in less than half a minute more he was committing the same offence again. "It isn't no use," he said, "I'm that sleepy you never seen."

"Then let's both take the watch below i'stead," said Philip, and they proceeded to stretch themselves out by the fire together.

"Just lave it to me," said Pete; "I'll hear them if they come in the night. I'll always does. I'm sleeping that light it's shocking. Why, sometimes I hear Black Tom when he comes home tipsy. I've done it times."

"We'll have carpets to lie on to-morrow, not stones," said Philip, wriggling on a rough one; "rolls of carpets—kidaminstrel ones."

They settled themselves side by side as close to each other as they could creep, and tried not to hear the surging and sighing of the sea. Then came a tremulous whimper:

"Pete!"

"What's that?"

"Don't you never say your prayers when you take the watch below?"

"Sometimes we does, when mother isn't too tired, and the ould man's middling drunk and quiet."

"Then don't you like to then?"

"Aw, yes, though, I'm liking it scandalous."

The wreckers agreed to say their prayers, and got up again and said them, knee to knee, with their two little faces to the fire, and then stretched themselves out afresh.

"Pete, where's your hand?"

"Here you are, Phil."

In another minute, under the solemn darkness of the night, broken only by the smouldering fire, amid the thunderous quake of the cavern after every beat of the waves on the beach, the Carrasdhoo men were asleep.

Sometime in the dark reaches before the dawn Pete leapt up with a start "What's that?" he cried, in a voice of fear.

But Philip was still in the mists of sleep, and, feeling the cold, he only whimpered, "Cover me up, Pete."

"Phil!" cried Pete, in an affrighted whisper.

"Cover me up," drawled Philip.

"I thought it was Black Tom," said Pete.

There was some confused bellowing outside the cave.

"My goodness grayshers!" came in a terrible voice, "it's them, though, the pair of them! Impozzible! who says it's impozzible? It's themselves I'm telling you, ma'm. Guy heng! The woman's mad, putting a scream out of herself like yonder. Safe? Coorse they're safe, bad luck to the young wastrels! You're for putting up a prayer for your own one. Eh? Well, I'm for hommering mine. The dirts? Weaned only yesterday, and fetching a dacent man out of his bed to find them. A fire at them, too! Well, it was the fire that found them. Pull the boat up, boys."

Philip was half awake by this time. "They've come," he whispered. "The ships is come, they're on the reef. Oh, dear me! Best go and meet them. P'raps they won't kill us if—if we—Oh, dear me!"

Then the wreckers, hand in hand, quaking and whimpering, stepped out to the mouth of the cave. At the next moment Philip found himself snatched up into the arms of Aunty Nan, who kissed him and cried over him, and rammed a great chunk of sweet cake into his cheek. Pete was faring differently. Under the leathern belt of Black Tom, who was thrashing him for both of them, he was howling like the sea in a storm.

Thus the Carrasdhoo men came home by the light of early morning—Pete skipping before the belt and bellowing; and Philip holding a piece of the cake at his teeth to comfort him.

IV

Philip left home for school at King William's by Castletown, and then Pete had a hard upbringing. His mother was tender enough, and there were good souls like Aunty Nan to show pity to both of them. But life went like a springless bogey, nevertheless. Sin itself is often easier than simpleness to pardon and condone. It takes a soft heart to feel tenderly towards a soft head.

Poor Pete's head seemed soft enough and to spare. No power and no persuasion could teach him to read and write. He went to school at the old schoolhouse by the church in Maughold village. The schoolmaster was a little man called John Thomas Corlett, pert and proud, with the sharp nose of a pike and the gait of a bantam. John Thomas was also a tailor. On a cowhouse door laid across two school forms he sat cross-legged among his cloth, his "maidens," and his smoothing irons, with his boys and girls, class by class, in a big half circle round about him.

The great little man had one standing ground of daily assault on the dusty jacket of poor Pete, and that was that the lad came late to school. Every morning Pete's welcome from the tailor-schoolmaster was a volley of expletives, and a swipe of the cane across his shoulders. "The craythur! The dunce! The durt! I'm taiching him, and taiching him, and he won't be taicht."

The soul of the schoolmaster had just two human weaknesses. One of these was a weakness for drink, and as a little vessel he could not take much without being full. Then he always taught the Church catechism and swore at his boys in Manx.

"Peter Quilliam," he cried one day, "who brought you out of the land of Egypt and the house of bondage?"

"'Deed, master," said Pete, "I never was in no such places, for I never had the money nor the clothes for it, and that's how stories are getting about."

The second of the schoolmaster's frailties was love of his daughter, a child of four, a cripple, whom he had lamed in her infancy, by letting her fall as he tossed her in his arms while in drink. The constant terror of his mind was lest some further accident should befall her. Between class and class he would go to a window, from which, when he had thrown up its lower sash, dim with the scratches of names, he could see one end of his own white cottage, and the little pathway, between lines of gilvers, coming down from the porch.

Pete had seen the little one hobbling along this path on her lame leg, and giggling with a heart of glee when she had eluded the eyes of her mother and escaped into the road. One day it chanced, after the heavy spring rains had swollen every watercourse, that he came upon the little curly poll, tumbling and tossing like a bell-buoy in a gale, down the flood of the river that runs to the sea at Port Mooar. Pete rescued the child and took her home, and then, as if he had done nothing unusual, he went on to school, dripping water from his legs at every step.

When John Thomas saw him coming, in bare feet, triddle-traddle, triddle-traddle, up the school-house floor, his indignation at the boy for being later than usual rose to fiery wrath for being drenched as well. Waiting for no explanation, concluding that Pete had been fishing for crabs among the stones of Port Lewaigue, he burst into a loud volley of his accustomed expletives, and timed and punctuated them by a thwack of the cane between every word.

"The waistrel! (thwack). The dirt! (thwack). I'm taiching him (thwack), and taiching him (thwack), and he won't be taicht!" (Thwack, thwack, thwack.)

Pete said never a word. Boiling his stinging shoulders under his jacket, and ramming his smarting hands, like wet eels, into his breeches' pockets, he took his place in silence at the bottom of the class.

But a girl, a little dark thing in a red frock, stepped out from her place beside the boy, shot up like a gleam to the schoolmaster as he returned to his seat among the cloth and needles, dealt him a smart slap across the face, and then burst into a lit of hysterical crying. Her name was Katherine Cregeen. She was the daughter of Cæsar the Cornaa miller, the founder of Ballajora Chapel, and a mighty man among the Methodists.

Katherine went unpunished, but that was the end of Pete's schooling. His learning was not too heavy for a big lad's head to carry—a bit of reading if it was all in print, and no writing at all except half-a-dozen capital letters. It was not a formidable equipment for the battle of life, but Bridget would not hear of more.

She herself, meanwhile, had annexed that character which was always the first and easiest to attach itself to a woman with a child but no visible father for it—the character of a witch. That name for his mother was Pete's earliest recollection of the high-road, and when the consciousness of its meaning came to him, he did not rebel, but sullenly acquiesced, for he had been born to it and knew nothing to the contrary. If the boys quarrelled with him at play, the first word was "your mother's a butch." Then he cried at the reproach, or perhaps fought like a vengeance at the insult, but he never dreamt of disbelieving the fact or of loving his mother any the less.

Bridget was accused of the evil eye. Cattle sickened in the fields, and when there was no proof that she had looked over the gate, the idea was suggested that she crossed them as a hare. One day a neighbour's dog started a hare in a meadow where some cows were grazing. This was observed by a gang of boys playing at hockey in the road. Instantly there was a shout and a whoop, and the boys with their sticks were in full chase after the yelping dog, crying, "The butch! The butch! It's Bridget Tom! Corlett's dogs are hunting Bridget Black Tom! Kill her, Laddie! Kill her, Sailor! Jump, dog, jump!"

One of the boys playing at hockey was Pete. When his play-fellows ran after the dogs in their fanatic thirst, he ran too, but with a storm of other feelings. Outstripping all of them, very close at the heels of the dogs, kicking some, striking others with the hockey-stick, while the tears poured down his cheeks, he cried at the top of his voice to the hare leaping in front, "Run, mammy, run! clink (dodge), mammy, clink! Aw, mammy, mammy, run faster, run for your life, run!"

The hare dodged aside, shot into a thicket, and escaped its pursuers just as Corlett, the farmer, who had heard the outcry, came racing up with a gun. Then Pete swept his coat-sleeve across his gleaming eyes and leapt off home. When he got there, he found his mother sitting on the bink by the door knitting quietly. He threw himself into her arms and stroked her cheek with his hand.

"Oh, mammy, bogh," he cried, "how well you run! If you never run in your life you run then."

"Is the boy mad?" said Bridget.

But Pete went on stroking her cheek and crying between sobs of joy, "I heard Corlett shouting to the house for a gun and a fourpenny bit, and I thought I was never going to see mammy no more. But you did clink, mammy! You did, though!"

The next time Katherine Cregeen saw Peter Quilliam, he was sitting on the ridge of rock at the mouth of Ballure Glen, playing doleful strains on a home-made whistle, and looking the picture of desolation and despair.

His mother was lying near to death. He had left Mrs. Cregeen, Kath-erine's mother, a good soul getting the name of Grannie, to watch and tend her while he came out to comfort his simple heart in this lone spot between the land and the sea.

Katherine's eyes filled at sight of him, and when, without looking up or speaking, he went on to play his crazy tunes, something took the girl by the throat and she broke down utterly.

"Never mind, Pete. No—I don't mean that—but don't cry, Pete."

Pete was not crying at all, but only playing away on his whistle and gazing out to sea with a look of dumb vacancy. Katherine knelt beside him, put her arms around his neck, and cried for both of them.

Somebody hailed him from the hedge by the water-trough, and he rose, took off his cap, smoothed his hair with his hand, and walked towards the house without a word.

Bridget was dying of pleurisy, brought on by a long day's work at hoeing turnips in a soaking rain. Dr. Mylechreest had poulticed her lungs with mustard and linseed, but all to no purpose. "It's feeling the same as the sun on your back at harvest," she murmured, yet the poultices brought no heat to her frozen chest.

Cæsar Cregeen was at her side; John the Clerk, too, called John the Widow; Kelly, the rural postman, who went by the name of Kelly the Thief; as well as Black Tom, her father. Cæsar was discoursing of sinners and their latter end. John was remembering how at his election to the clerkship he had rashly promised to bury the poor for nothing; Kelly was thinking he would be the first to carry the news to Christian Balla-whaine; and Black Tom was varying the exercise of pounding rock-sugar for his bees with that of breaking his playful wit on the dying woman.

"No use; I'm laving you; I'm going on my long journey," said Bridget, while Granny used a shovel as a fan to relieve her gusty breathing.

"Got anything in your pocket for the road, woman?" said the thatcher.

"It's not houses of bricks and mortal I'm for calling at now," she answered.

"Dear heart! Put up a bit of a prayer," whispered Grannie to her husband; and Cæsar took a pinch of snuff out of his waistcoat pocket, and fell to "wrastling with the Lord."

Bridget seemed to be comforted. "I see the jasper gates," she panted, fixing her hazy eyes on the scraas under the thatch, from which broken spiders' webs hung down like rats' tails.

Then she called for Pete. She had something to give him. It was the stocking foot with the eighty greasy Manx banknotes which his father, Peter Christian, had paid her fifteen years before. Pete lit the candle and steadied it while Grannie cut the stocking from the wall side of the bed-ticking.

Black Tom dropped the sugar-pounder and exposed his broken teeth in his surprise at so much wealth; John the Widow blinked; and Kelly the Thief poked his head forward until the peak of his postman's cap fell on to the bridge of his nose.

A sea-fog lay over the land that morning, and when it lifted Bridget's soul went up as well.

"Poor thing! Poor thing!" said Grannie. "The ways were cold for her—cold, cold!"

"A dacent lass," said John the Clerk; "and oughtn't to be buried with the common trash, seeing she's left money."

"A hard-working woman, too, and on her feet for ever; but 'lowanced in her intellecks, for all," said Kelly.

And Cæsar cried, "A brand plucked from the burning! Lord, give me more of the like at the judgment."

When all was over, and tears both hot and cold were wiped away—Pete shed none of them—the neighbours who had stood with the lad in the churchyard on Maughold Head returned to the cottage by the water-trough to decide what was to be done with his eighty good bank-notes. "It's a fortune," said one. "Let him put it with Mr. Dumbell," said another. "Get the boy a trade first—he's a big lump now, sixteen for spring," said a third. "A draper, eh?" said a fourth. "May I presume? My nephew, Bobbie Clucas, of Ramsey, now?" "A dacent man, very," said John the Widow; "but if I'm not ambitious, there's my son-in-law, John Cowley. The lad's cut to a dot for a grocer, and what more nicer than having your own shop and your own name over the door, if you plaze—' Peter Quilliam, tay and sugar merchant!'—they're telling me John will be riding in his carriage and pair soon."

"Chut! your grannie and your carriage and pairs," shouted a rasping voice at last. It was Black Tom. "Who says the fortune is belonging to the lad at all? It's mine, and if there's law in the land I'll have it."

Meanwhile, Pete, with the dull thud in his ears of earth falling on a coffin, had made his way down to Ballawhaine. He had never been there before, and he felt confused, but he did not tremble. Half-way up the carriage-drive he passed a sandy-haired youth of his own age, a slim dandy who hummed a tune and looked at him carelessly over his shoulder. Pete knew him—he was Boss, the boys called him Dross, son and heir of Christian Ballawhaine.

At the big house Pete asked for the master. The English footman, in scarlet knee-breeches, left him to wait in the stone hall. The place was very quiet and rather cold, but all as clean as a gull's wing. There was a dark table in the middle and a high-backed chair against the wall. Two oil pictures faced each other from opposite sides. One was of an old man without a beard, but with a high forehead, framed around with short grey hair. The other was of a woman with a tired look and a baby on her lap. Under this there was a little black picture that seemed to Pete to be the likeness of a fancy tombstone. And the print on it, so far as Pete could spell it out, was that of a tombstone too, "In loving memory of Verbena, beloved wife of Peter Chr—"

The Ballawhaine came crunching the sand on the hall-floor. He looked old, and had now a pent-house of bristly eyebrows of a different colour from his hair. Pete had often seen him on the road riding by.

"Well, my lad, what can I do for *you?*" he said. He spoke in a jerky voice, as if he thought to overawe the boy.

Pete fumbled his stocking cap. "Mothers dead," he answered vacantly.

The Ballawhaine knew that already. Kelly the Thief had run hot-foot to inform him. He thought Pete had come to claim maintenance now that his mother was gone.

"So she's been telling you the same old story?" he said briskly.

At that Pete's face stiffened all at once. "She's been telling me that you're my father, sir."

The Ballawhaine tried to laugh. "Indeed!" he replied; "it's a wise child, now, that knows its own father."

"I'm not rightly knowing what you mane, sir," said Pete.

Then the Ballawhaine fell to slandering the poor woman in her grave, declaring that she could not know who was the father of her child, and protesting that no son of hers should ever see the colour of money of his. Saying this with a snarl, he brought down his right hand with a thump on to the table. There was a big hairy mole near the joint of the first finger.

"Aisy, sir, if you plaze," said Pete; "she was telling me you gave her this."

He turned up the corner of his jersey, tugged out of his pocket, from behind his flaps, the eighty Manx bank-notes, and held them in his right hand on the table. There was a mole at the joint of Pete's first finger also.

The Ballawhaine saw it. He drew back his hand and slid it behind him. Then in another voice he said, "Well, my lad, isn't it enough? What are you wanting with more?"

"I'm not wanting more," said Pete; "I'm not wanting this. Take it back," and he put down the roll of notes between them.

The Ballawhaine sank into the chair, took a handkerchief out of his tails with the hand that had been lurking there, and began to mop his forehead. "Eh? How? What d'ye mean, boy?" he stammered.

"I mane," said Pete, "that if I kept that money there is people would say my mother was a bad woman, and you bought her and paid her—I'm hearing the like at some of them."

He took a step nearer. "And I mane, too, that you did wrong by my mother long ago, and now that she's dead you're blackening her; and you're a bad heart, and a low tongue, and if I was only a man, and didn't *know* you were my father, I'd break every bone in your skin."

Then Pete twisted about and shouted into the dark part of the hall, "Come along, there, my ould cockatoo! It's time to be putting me to the door."

The English footman in the scarlet breeches had been peeping from under the stairs.

That was Pete's first and last interview with his father. Peter Christian Ballawhaine was a terror in the Keys by this time, but he had trembled before his son like a whipped cur.

V

Katherine Cregeen, Pete's champion at school, had been his companion at home as well. She was two years younger than Pete. Her hair was a black as a gipsy's, and her face as brown as a berry. In summer she liked best to wear a red frock without sleeves, no boots and no stockings, no collar and no bonnet, not even a sun-bonnet. From constant exposure to the sun and rain her arms and legs were as ruddy as her cheeks, and covered with a soft silken down. So often did you see her teeth that you would have said she was always laughing. Her laugh was a little saucy trill given out with head aside and eyes aslant, like that of a squirrel when he is at a safe height above your head, and has a nut in his open jaws.

Pete had seen her first at school, and there he had tried to draw the eyes of the maiden upon himself by methods known only to heroes, to savages, and to boys. He had prowled around her in the playground with the wild vigour of a young colt, tossing his head, swinging his arms, screwing his body, kicking up his legs, walking on his hands, lunging out at every lad that was twice as big as himself, and then bringing himself down at length with a whoop and a crash on his hindmost parts just in front of where she stood. For these tremendous efforts to show what a fellow he could be if he tried, he had won no applause from the boys, and Katherine herself had given no sign, though Pete had watched her out of the corners of his eyes. But in other scenes the children came together.

After Philip had gone to King William's, Pete and Katherine had become bosom friends. Instead of going home after school to cool his heels in the road until his mother came from the fields, he found it neighbourly to go up to Ballajora and round by the network of paths to Cornaa. That was a long detour, but Cæsar's mill stood there. It nestled down in the low bed of the river that runs through the glen called Ballaglass.

Song-birds built about it in the spring of the year, and Cæsar's little human songster sang there always.

When Pete went that way home, what times the girl had of it! Wading up the river, clambering over the stones, playing female Blondin on the fallen tree-trunks that spanned the chasm, slipping, falling, holding on any way up (legs or arms) by the rotten branches below, then calling for Pete's help in a voice between a laugh and a cry, flinging chips into the foaming back-wash of the mill-wheel, and chasing them down stream, racing among the gorse, and then lying full length like a lamb, without a thought of shame, while Pete took the thorns out of her bleeding feet. She was a wild duck in the glen where she lived, and Pete was a great lumbering tame duck waddling behind her.

But the glorious, happy, make-believe days too soon came to an end. The swinging cane of the great John Thomas Corlett, and the rod of a yet more relentless tyrant, darkened the sunshine of both the children. Pete was banished from school, and Catherine's father removed from Cornaa.

When Cæsar had taken a wife, he had married Betsy, the daughter of the owner of the inn at Sulby. After that he had "got religion," and he held that persons in the household of faith were not to drink, or to buy or to sell drink. But Grannie's father died and left his house, "The Manx Fairy," and his farm, Glenmooar, to her and her husband. About the same time the miller at Sulby also died, and the best mill in the island cried out for a tenant. Cæsar took the mill and the farm, and Grannie took the inn, being brought up to such profanities and no way bound by principle. From that time forward, Cæsar pinned all envious cavillers with the text which says, "Not that which goeth into the mouth of a man defileth him, but that which cometh out."

Nevertheless, Cæsar's principles grew more and more puritanical year by year. There were no half measures with Cæsar. Either a man was a saved soul, or he was in the very belly of hell, though the pit might not have shut its mouth on him. If a man was saved he knew it, and if he felt the manifestations of the Spirit he could live without sin. His cardinal principles were three—instantaneous regeneration, assurance, and sinless perfection. He always said—he had said it a thousand times—that he was converted in Douglas marketplace, a piece off the west door of ould St. Matthew's, at five-and-twenty minutes past six on a Sabbath evening in July, when he was two-and-twenty for harvest.

While at Cornaa, Cæsar had been a "local" on the preachers' plan, a class leader, and a chapel steward; but at Sulby he outgrew the Union and set up a "body" of his own. He called them "The Christians." a title that was at once a name, a challenge, and a protest. They worshipped in the long barn over Cæsar's mill, and held strong views on conduct. A saved soul must not wear gold or costly apparel, or give way to softness or bodily indulgence, or go to fairs for sake of sport, or appear in the show-tents of play-actors, or sing songs, or read books, or take any diversion that did not tend to the knowledge of God. As for carnal transgression, if any were guilty of it, they were to be cut off from the body of believers, for the souls of the righteous must be delivered.

"The religion that's going among the Primitives these days is just Popery," said Cæsar. "Let's go back to the warm ould Methodism and put out the Romans."

When Pete turned his face from Ballawhaine, he thought first of Cæsar and his mill. It would be more exact to say he thought of Katherine and Grannie. He was homeless as well as penniless. The cottage by the water-trough was no longer possible to him, now that the mother was gone who had stood between his threatened shoulders and Black Tom. Philip was at home for a few weeks only in the year, and Ballure had lost its attraction. So Pete made his way to Sulby, offered himself to Cæsar for service at the mill, and was taken on straightway at eighteenpence a week and his board.

It was a curious household he entered into. First there was Cæsar himself, in a moleskin waistcoat with sleeves open three buttons up, knee-breeches usually unlaced, stockings of undyed wool, and slippers with the tongues hanging out—a grim soul, with whiskers like a hoop about his face, and a shaven upper lip as heavy as a moustache, for, when religion like Cæsar's lays hold of a man, it takes him first by the mouth. Then Grannie, a comfortable body in a cap, with an outlook on life that was all motherhood, a simple, tender, peaceable soul, agreeing with everybody and everything, and seeming to say nothing but "Poor thing! Poor thing!" and "Dear heart! Dear heart!" Then there was Nancy Cain, getting the name of Nancy Joe, the servant in name but the mistress in fact, a niece of Grannie's, a bit of a Pagan, an early riser, a tireless worker, with a plain face, a rooted disbelief in all men, a good heart, an ugly tongue, and a vixenish temper. Last of all, there was Katherine, now grown to be a great girl, with her gipsy hair done up in a red ribbon and wearing a black pinafore bordered with white braid.

Pete got on steadily at the mill. He began by lighting the kiln fire and cleaning out the pit-wheel, and then on to the opening the flood-gates in the morning and regulating the action of the water-wheel according to the work of the day. In two years' time he was a sound miller, safe to trust with rough stuff for cattle or fine flour for white loaf-bread. Cæsar trusted him. He would take evangelising journeys to Peel or Douglas and leave Pete in charge.

That led to the end of the beginning. Pete could grind the farmers' corn, but he could not make their reckonings. He kept his counts in chalk on the back of the mill-house door, a down line for every stone weight up to eight stones, and a line across for every hundredweight. Then, once a day, while the father was abroad, Katherine came over from the inn to the desk at the little window of the mill, and turned Pete's lines into ledger accounts. These financial councils were full of delicious discomfiture. Pete always enjoyed them—after they were over.

"John Robert—Molleycarane—did you say Molleycarane, Pete? Oh, Mylecharane—Myle-c-h-a-r-a-i-n-e, Molleycarane; ten stones—did you say ten? Oh, eight—e-i-g-h-t—no, eight; oatmeal, Pete? Oh, barley-male—meal, I mean—m-e-a-l."

In the middle of the night Pete remembered all these entries. They were very precious to his memory after Katherine had spoken them. They sang in his heart the same as song-birds then. They were like hymns and tunes and pieces of poetry.

Cæsar returned home from a preaching tour with a great and sudden thought. He had been calling on strangers to flee from the wrath to come, and yet there were those of his own house whose faces were not turned Zionwards. That evening he held an all-night prayer-meeting for the conversion of Katherine and Pete. Through six long hours he called on God in lusty tones, until his throat cracked and his forehead streamed. The young were thoughtless, they had the root of evil in them, they flew into frivolity from contrariness. Draw the harrow over their souls, plough the fallows of their hearts, grind the chaff out of their household, let not the sweet apple and the crabs grow on the same bough together, give them a Melliah, let not a sheaf be forgotten, grant them the soul of this girl for a harvest-home, and of this boy for a last stook.

Cæsar was dissatisfied with the results. He was used to groaning and trembling and fainting fits.

"Don't you feel the love?" he cried. "I do—here, under the watch-pocket of my waistcoat."

Towards midnight Katherine began to fail. "Chain the devil,", cried Cæsar. "Once I was down in the pit with the devil myself, but now I'm up in the loft, seeing angels through the thatch. Can't you feel the workings of the Spirit?"

As the clock was warning to strike two Katherine thought she could, and from that day forward she led the singing of the women in the choir among "The Christians."

Pete remained among the unregenerate; but nevertheless "The Christians" saw him constantly. He sat on the back form and kept his eyes fixed on the "singing seat." Observing his regularity, Cæsar laid a hand on his head and told him the Spirit was working in his soul at last. Sometimes Pete thought it was, and that was when he shut his eyes and listened to

Katherine's voice floating up, up, up, like an angel's, into the sky. But sometimes he knew it was not; and that was when he caught himself in the middle of Cæsar's mightiest prayers crooking his neck past the pitching bald pate of Johnny Niplightly, the constable, that he might get a glimpse of the top of Katherine's bonnet when her eyes were down.

Pete fell into a melancholy, and once more took to music as a comforter. It was not a home-made whistle now, but a fiddle bought out of his wages. On this he played in the cowhouse on winter evenings, and from the top of the midden outside in summer. When Cæsar heard of it his wrath was fearful. What was a fiddler? He was a servant of corruption, holding a candle to disorderly walkers and happy sinners on their way into the devil's pinfold. And what for was fiddles? Fiddles was for play-actors and theaytres. "And theaytres is *there*," said Cæsar, indicating with his foot one flag on the kitchen-floor, "and hell flames is *there*," he added, rolling his toe over to the joint of the next one.

Grannie began to plead. What was a fiddle if you played the right tunes on it? Didn't they read in the ould Book of King David himself playing on harps and timbrels and such things? And what was harps but fiddles in a way of spak-ing? Then warn't they all looking to be playing harps in heaven? 'Deed, yes, though the Lord would have to be teaching her how to play hers!

Cæsar was shaken. "Well, of course, certainly," he said, "if there's a power in fiddling to bring souls out of bondage, and if there's going to be fiddling and the like in Abraham's bosom—why, then, of course—well, why not?—let's have the lad's fiddle up at 'The Christians.'"

Nothing could have suited Pete so well. From that time forward he went out no more at nights to the cowhouse, but stayed indoors to practise hymns with Katherine. Oh, the terrible rapture of those nightly "practices!" They brought people to the inn to hear them, and so Cæsar found them good for profit both ways.

There was something in Cæsar's definition, nevertheless. It was found that among the saints there were certain weaker brethren who did not want a hymn to their ale. One of these was Johnny Niplightly, the rural constable, who was the complement of Katherine in the choir, being leader of the singing among the men. He was a tall man with a long nose, which seemed to have a perpetual cold. Making his rounds one night, he turned in at "The Manx Fairy," when Cæsar and Grannie were both from home, and Nancy Joe was in charge, and Pete and Katherine were practising a revival chorus.

"Where's Cæsar, dough?" he snuffled.

"At Peel, buying the stock," snapped Nancy.

"Dank de Lord! I mean—where's Grannie?"

"Nursing Mistress Quiggin."

Niplightly eased the strap of his beaver, liberated his lips, took a deep draught of ale, and then turned to Pete, with apologetic smiles, and suggested a change in the music.

At that Katherine leapt up as light as laughter. "A dance," she cried, "a dance!"

"Good sakes alive?" said Nancy Joe. "Listen to the girl? Is it the moon, Kitty, or what is it that's doing on you?"

"Shut your eyes, Nancy," said Katherine, "just for once, now won't you?"

"You can do what you like with me, with your coaxing and woaxing," said Nancy. "Enjoy yourself to the full, girl, but don't make a noise above the singing of the kettle."

Pete tuned his strings, and Katherine pinned up the tail of her skirt, and threw herself into position.

At the sound of the livelier preludings there came thronging out of the road into the parlour certain fellows of the baser sort, and behind them came one who was not of that denomination—a fair young man with a fine face under an Alpine hat. Heeding nothing of this audience, the girl gave a little rakish toss of her head and called on Pete to strike up.

Then Pete plunged into one of the profaner tunes which he had practised in the days of the cowhouse, and off went Katherine with a whoop. The boys stood back for her, bending down on their haunches as at a fight of gamecocks, and encouraging her with shouts of applause.

"Beautiful! Look at that now! Fine, though, fine! Clane done, aw, clane! Done to a dot! There's leaping for you, boys! Guy heng, did you ever see the like? Hommer the floor, girl—higher a piece! higher, then! Whoop, did ye ever see such a nate pair of ankles?"

"Hould your dirty tongue, you gobmouthed omathaun!" cried Nancy Joe. She had tried to keep her eyes away, but could not. "My goodness grayshers!" she cried. "Did you ever see the like, though? Screwing like the windmill on the schoolhouse! Well, well, Kitty, woman! Aw, Kirry, Kirry! Wherever did she get it, then? Goodsakes, the girl's twisting herself into knots!"

Pete was pulling away at the fiddle with both hands, like a bottom sawyer, his eyes dancing, his lips quivering, the whole soul of the lad lifted out of himself in an instant.

"Hould on still, Kate, hould on, girl!" he shouted. "Ma-chree! Machree! The darling's dancing like a drumstick!"

"Faster!" cried Kate. "Faster!"

The red ribbon had fallen from her head, and the wavy black hair was tumbling about her face. She was holding up her skirt with one hand, and the other arm was akimbo at her waist. Guggling, chuckling, crowing, panting, boiling, and bubbling with the animal life which all her days had been suppressed, and famished and starved into moans and groans, she was carried away by her own fire, gave herself up to it, and danced on the flags of the kitchen which had served Cæsar for his practical typology, like a creature intoxicated with new breath.

Meantime Cæsar himself, coming home in his chapel hat (his tall black beaver) from Peel, where he had been buying the year's stock of herrings at the boat's side, had overtaken, on the road, the venerable parson of his parish, Parson Quiggin of Lezayre. Drawing up the gig with a "Woa!" he had invited the old clergyman to a lift by his side on the gig's seat, which was cushioned with a sack of hay. The parson had accepted the invitation, and with a preliminary "Aisy! Your legs a taste higher, sir, just to keep the pickle off your trousers," a "Gee up!" and a touch of the whip, they were away together, with the light of the gig-lamp on the hind-quarters of the mare, as they bobbed and screwed like a mill-race under the splash-hoard.

It was Cæsar's chance, and he took it. Having pinned one of the heads of the Church, he gave him his views on the Romans, and on the general encroachment of Popery. The parson listened complacently. He was a tolerant old soul, with a round face, expressive of perpetual happiness, though he was always blinking his little eyes and declaring, with the Preacher, that all earthly things were vain. Hence he was nicknamed Old Vanity of Vanities.

The gig had swept past Sulby Chapel when Cæsar began to ask for the parson's opinion of certain texts.

"And may I presume, Pazon Quiggin, what d'ye think of the text—'Praise the Lord. O my soul, and all that is within me praise His Holy Name?'"

"A very good text after meat, Mr. Cregeen," said the parson, blinking his little eyes in the dark.

It was Cæsar's favourite text, and his fire was kindled at the parson's praise. "Man alive," he cried, his hot breath tickling the parson's neck, "I've praiched on that text, pazon, till it's wet me through to the waistcoat."

They were near to "The Manx Fairy" by this time.

"And talking of praise," said Cæsar, "I hear them there at their practices. Asking pardon now—it's proud I'd be, sir—perhaps you'd not be thinking mane to come in and hear the way we do 'Crown Him!'"

"So the saints use the fiddle," said the parson, as the gig drew up at the porch of the inn.

Half a minute afterwards the door of the parlour flew open with a bang, and Cæsar stood and glared on the threshold with the parson's ruddy face behind him. There was a moment's silence. The uplifted toe of Katherine trailed back to the ground, the fiddle of Pete slithered to his farther side, and the smacking lips of Niplightly transfixed themselves agape. Then the voice of the parson was heard to say, "Vanity, vanity, all is vanity!" and suddenly Cæsar, still on the threshold, went down on his knees to pray.

Cæsar's prayer was only a short one. His mortified pride called for quicker solace. Rising to his feet with as much dignity as he could command under the twinkling eyes of the parson, he stuttered, "The capers! Making a dacent house into a theaytre! Respectable person, too—one of the first that's going! So," facing the spectators, "just help yourselves home the pack of you! As for these ones," turning on Kate, Pete, and the constable, "there'll be no more of your practices. I'll do without the music of three saints like you. In future I'll have three sinners to raise my singing. These polices, too!" he said with a withering smile. (Niplightly was worming his way out at the back of Parson Quiggin.)

"Who began it?" shouted Cæsar, looking at Katherine.

From the moment that Cæsar dropped on his knees at the door, Pete had been well-nigh choked by an impulse to laugh aloud. But now he bit his lip and said, "I did!"

"Behould ye now, as imperent as a goat!" said Cæsar, working his eyebrows vigorously. "You've mistaken your profession, boy. It's a play-actorer they ought to be making of you. You're wasting your time with a plain, respectable man like me. You must lave me. Away to the loft for your chiss, boy! And just give sheet, my lad, and don't lay to till you've fetched up at another lodgings."

Pete, with his eye on the parson's face, could control himself no longer, and he laughed so loud that the room rang.

"Right's the word, ould Nebucannezzar," he cried, and heaved up to his feet. "So long, Kitty, woman! S'long! We'll finish it another night though, and then the ould man himself will be houlding the candle."

Outside in the road somebody touched him on the shoulder. It was the young man in the Alpine hat.

"My gough! What? Phil!" cried Pete, and he laid hold of him with both hands at once.

"I've just finished at King William's and bought a boat," said Philip, "and I came up to ask you to join me—congers and cods, you know—good fun anyway. Are you willing?"

"Willing!" cried Pete. "Am I jumping for joy?"

And away they went down the road, swinging their legs together with a lively step.

"That's a nice girl, though—Kitty, Kate, what do you call her?" said Phil.

"Were you in then? So you saw her dancing?" said Pete eagerly. "Aw, yes, nice," he said warmly, "nice uncommon," he added absently, and then with a touch of sadness, "shocking nice!"

Presently they heard the pattering of light feet in the darkness behind them, and a voice like a broken cry calling "Pete!"

It was Kate. She came up panting and catching her breath in hiccoughs, took Pete's face in both her hands, drew it down to her own face, kissed it on the mouth, and was gone again without a word.

VI

Philip had not been a success at school; he had narrowly escaped being a failure. During his earlier years he had shown industry without gifts; during his later years he had shown gifts without industry. His childish saying became his by-word, and half in sport, half in earnest, with a smile on his lips, and a shuddering sense of fascination, he would say when the wind freshened, "The sea's calling me, I must be off." The blood of the old sea-dog, his mother's father, was strong in him. Idleness led to disaster, and disaster to some disgrace. He was indifferent to both while at school, but shame found him out at home.

"You'll be sixteen for spring," said Auntie Nan, "and what would your poor father say if he were alive? He thought worlds of his boy, and always said what a man he would be some day."

That was the shaft that found Philip. The one passion that burned in his heart like a fire was reverence for the name and the will of his dead father. The big hopes of the broken man had sometimes come as a torture to the boy when the blood of the old salt was rioting within him. But now they came as a spur.

Philip went back to school and worked like a slave. There were only three terms left, and it was too late for high honours, but the boy did wonders. He came out well, and the masters were astonished. "After all," they said, "there's no denying it, the boy Christian must have the gift of genius. There's nothing he might not do."

If Phil had much of the blood of Captain Billy, Pete had much of the blood of Black Tom. After leaving the mill at Sulby, Pete made his home in the cabin of the smack. What he was to eat, and how he was to be clothed, and where he was to be lodged when the cold nights came, never troubled his mind for an instant. He had fine times with his partner. The terms of their partnership were simple. Phil took the fun and made Pete take the fish. They were a pair of happy-go-lucky lads, and they looked to the future with cheerful faces.

There was one shadow over their content, and that was the ghost of a gleam of sunshine. It made daylight between them, though, day by day as they ran together like two that run a race. The prize was Katherine Cregeen. Pete talked of her till Phil's heart awoke and trembled; but Phil hardly knew it was so, and Pete never once suspected it. Neither confessed to the other, and the shifts of both to hide the secret of each were boyish and beautiful.

There is a river famous for trout that rises in Sulby glen and flows into Ramsey harbour. One of the little attempts of the two lads to deceive each other was to make believe that it was their duty to fish this river with the rod, and so wander away singly up the banks of the stream until they came to "The Manx Fairy," and then drop in casually to quench the thirst of so much angling. Towards the dusk of evening Philip, in a tall silk hat over a jacket and knickerbockers, would come upon Pete by the Sulby bridge, washed, combed, and in a collar. Then there would be looks of great surprise on both sides. "What, Phil! Is it yourself, though? Just thought I'd see if the trouts were biting to-night. Dear me, this is Sulby too! And bless my soul, 'The Fairy' again I Well, a drop of drink will do no harm. Shall we put a sight on them inside, eh?" After that prelude they would go into the house together.

This little comedy was acted every night for weeks. It was acted on Hollantide Eve six months after Pete had been turned out by Cæsar. Grannie was sitting by the glass partition, knitting at intervals, serving at the counter occasionally and scoring up on a black board that was a mass of chalk hieroglyphics. Cæsar himself in ponderous spectacles and with a big book in his hands was sitting in the kitchen behind with his back to the glass, so as to make the lamp of the business serve also for his studies. On a bench in the bar sat Black Tom, smoking, spitting, scraping his feet on the sanded floor, and looking like a gigantic spider with enormous bald head. At his side was a thin man with a face pitted by smallpox, and a forehead covered with strange protuberances. This was Jonaique Jelly, barber, clock-mender, and Manx patriot. The postman was there, too, Kelly the Thief, a tiny creature with twinkling ferret eyes, and a face that had a settled look of age, as of one born old, being wrinkled in squares like the pointing of a cobble wall.

At sight of Pete, Grannie made way, and he pushed through to the kitchen, where he seated himself in a seat in the fireplace just in front of the peat closet, and under the fish hanging to smoke. At sight of Phil she dropped her needles, smoothed her front hair, rose in spite of protest, and wiped down a chair by the ingle. Cæsar eyed Pete in silence from between the top rim of his spectacles and the bottom edge of the big book; but as Philip entered he lowered the book and welcomed him. Nancy Joe was coming and going in her clogs like a rip-rap let loose between the dairy and a pot of potatoes in their jackets which swung from the slowrie, the hook over the fire. A moment later Kate came flitting through the half-lit kitchen, her black eyes dancing and her mouth rippling in smiles. She courtesied to Philip, grimaced at Pete, and disappeared.

Then from the other side of the glass partition came the husky voice of the postman, saying, "Well, I must be taking the road, gentlemen. There's Manx ones starting for Kim-berley by the early sailing to-morrow morning."

And then came the voice of the barber in a hoarse falsetto: "Kimberley! That's the place for good men I'm always saying. There's Billy the Red back home with a fortune. And ould Corlett—look at ould Corlett, the Ballabeg! Five years away at the diggings, and left a house worth twenty pounds per year per annum, not to spake of other hereditaments."

After that the rasping voice of Black Tom, in a tone of irony and contempt: "Of coorse, aw, yes, of coorse, there's goold on the cushags there, they're telling me. But I thought you were a man that's all for the island, Mr. Jelly."

"Lave me alone for that," said the voice of the barber. "Manx-land for the Manx-man—that's the text I'm houlding to. But what's it saying, 'Custom must be indulged with custom, or custom will die?' And with these English scouring over it like puffins on the Calf, it isn't much that's left of the ould island but the name. The best of the Manx boys are going away foreign, same as these ones."

"Well, I've letters for them to the packet-office anyway," said the postman.

"Who are they, Mr. Kelly?" called Philip, through the doorway.

"Some of the Quarks ones from Glen Rushen, sir, and the Gills boys from Castletown over. Good-night all, goodnight!"

The door closed behind the postman, and Black Tom growled, "Slips of lads—I know them."

"Smart though, smart uncommon," said the barber; "that's the only sort they're wanting out yonder."

There was a contemptuous snort. "So? You'd better go to Kimberley yourself, then."

"Turn the clock back a piece and I'll start before you've time to curl your hair," said the barber.

Black Tom was lifting his pot. "That's the one thing," said he, "the Almighty Himself" (gulp, gulp) "can't do."

"Which?" tittered the barber.

"Both," said Black Tom, scratching his big head, as bald as a bladder.

Cæsar flashed about with his face to the glass partition. "You're like the rest of the infidels, sir," said he, "only spaking to contradick yourself— calling God the Almighty, and telling in the same breath of something He can't do."

Meanwhile an encounter of another sort was going on at the ingle. Kate had re-appeared with a table fork which she used at intervals to test the boiling of the potatoes. At each approach to the fire she passed close to where Pete sat, never looking at Phil above the level of his boots. And as often as she bent over the pot, Pete put his arm round her waist, being so near and so tempting. For thus pestering her she beat her foot like a goat, and screwed on a look of anger which broke down in a stifled laugh; but she always took care to come again to Pete's side rather than to Phil's, until at last the nudging and shoving ended in a pinch and a little squeal, and a quick cry of "What's that?" from Cæsar.

Kate vanished like a flash, the dim room began to frown again, and Phil to draw his breath heavily, when the girl came back as suddenly bringing an apple and a length of string. Mounting a chair, she fixed one end of the string to the lath of the ceiling by the peck, the parchment oatcake pan, and the other end she tied to the stalk of the apple.

"What's the jeel now?" said Pete.

"Fancy! Don't you know? Not heard f'Hop-tu-naa'? It's Hollantide Eve, man," said Kate.

Then setting the string going like a pendulum, she stood back a pace with hands clasped behind her, and snapped at the apple as it swung, sometimes catching it, sometimes missing it, sometimes marking it, sometimes biting it, her body bending and rising with its waggle, and nod, and bob, her mouth opening and closing, her white teeth gleaming, and her whole face bubbling over with delight. At every touch the speed increased, and the laughter grew louder as the apple went faster. Everybody, except the miller, joined in the fun. Phil cried out on the girl to look to her teeth, but Pete egged her on to test the strength of them.

"Snap at it, Kitty!" cried Pete. "Aw, lost! Lost again! Ow! One in the cheek! No matter! Done!"

And Black Tom and Mr. Jelly stood up to watch through the doorway. "My goodness grayshers!" cried one. "What a mouthful!" said the other. "Share it, Kitty, woman; aw, share and share alike, you know."

But then came the thunderous tones of Cæsar. "Drop it, drop it! Such practices is nothing but Popery."

"Popery!" cried Black Tom from over the counter. "Chut! nonsense, man! The like of it was going before St. Patrick was born."

Kate was puffing and panting and taking down the pendulum.

"What does it mean then, Tom?" she said; "it's you for knowing things."

"Mane? It manes fairies!"

"Fairies!"

Black Tom sat down with a complacent air, and his rasping voice came from the other side of the glass. "In the ould times gone by, girl, before Manxmen got too big for their breeches, they'd be off to bed by ten o'clock on Hollantide Eve to lave room for the little people that's outside to come in. And the big woman of the house would be filling the crocks for the fairies to drink, and the big man himself would be raking the ashes so they might bake their cakes, and a girl, same as you, would be going to bed backwards——"

"I know! I know!" cried Kate, near to the ceiling, and clapping her hands. "She eats a roasted apple, and goes to bed thirsty, and then dreams that somebody brings her a drink of water, and that's the one that's to be her husband, eh?"

"You've got it, girl."

Cæsar had been listening with his eyes turned sideways off his book, and now he cried, "Then drop it, I'm telling you. It's nothing but instruments of Satan, and the ones that's telling it are just flying in the face of faith from superstition and contrariety. It isn't dacent in a Christian public-house, and I'm for having no more of it."

Grannie paused in her knitting, fixed her cap with one of her needles and said, "Dear heart, father! Tom meant no harm." Then, glancing at the clock and rising, "But it's time to shut up the house, anyway. Good night, Tom! Good night all! Good night!"

Phil and Pete rose also. Pete went to the door and pretended to look out, then came back to Kate's side and whispered, "Come, give them the slip—there's somebody outside that's waiting for you."

"Let them wait," said the girl, but she laughed, and Pete knew she would come. Then he turned to Philip, "A word in your ear, Phil," he said, and took him by the arm and drew him out of the house and round to the yard of the stable.

"Well, good night, Grannie," said Mr. Jelly, going out behind them. "But if I were as young as your grandson there, Mr. Quilliam, I would be making a start for somewhere."

"Grandson!" grunted Tom, heaving up, "I've got no grandson, or he wouldn't be laving me to smoke a dry pipe. But he's making an Almighty of this Phil Christian—that's it."

After they were gone, Grannie began counting the till and saying, "As for fairies—one, two, three—it may be, as Cæsar says—four—five—the like isn't in, but it's safer to be civil to them anyway."

"Aw, yes," said Nancy Joe, "a crock of fresh water and a few good words going to bed on Hollantide Eve does no harm at all, at all."

Outside in the stable-yard the feet of Black Tom and Jonaique Jelly were heard going off on the road. The late moon was hanging low, red as an evening sun, over the hill to the south-east. Pete was puffing and blowing as if he had been running a race. "Quick, boy, quick!" he was whispering, "Kate's coming. A word in your ear first. Will you do me a turn, Phil?"

"What is it?" said Philip.

"Spake to the ould man for me while I spake to the girl!"

"What about?" said Philip.

But Pete could hear, nothing except his own voice. "The ould angel herself, she's all right, but the ould man's hard. Spake for me, Phil; you've got the fine English tongue at you."

"But what about?" Philip said again.

"Say I may be a bit of a rip, but I'm not such a bad sort anyway. Make me out a taste, Phil, and praise me up. Say I'll be as good as goold; yes, will I though. Tell him he has only to say yes, and I'll be that studdy and willing and hardworking and persevering you never seen."

"But, Pete, Pete, Pete, whatever am I to say all this about?"

Pete's puffing and panting ceased. "What about? Why, about the girl for sure."

"The girl!" said Philip.

"What else?" said Pete.

"Kate? Am I to speak for you to the father for Kate?"

Philip's voice seemed to come up from the bottom depths of his throat.

"Are you thinking hard of the job, Phil?"

There was a moment's silence. The blood had rushed to Philip's face, which was full of strange matter, but the darkness concealed it.

"I didn't say that," he faltered.

Pete mistook Philip's hesitation for a silent commentary on his own unworthiness. "I know I'm only a sort of a waistrel," he said, "but, Phil, the way I'm loving that girl it's shocking. I can never take rest for thinking of her. No, I'm not sleeping at night nor working reg'lar in the day neither. Everything is telling of her, and everything is shouting her name. It's 'Kate' in the sea, and 'Kate' in the river, and the trees and the gorse. 'Kate,' 'Kate,' 'Kate,' it's Kate constant, and I can't stand much more of it. I'm loving the girl scandalous, that's the truth, Phil."

Pete paused, but Philip gave no sign.

"It's hard to praise me, that's sarten sure," said Pete, "but I've known her since she was a little small thing in pinafores, and I was a slip of a big boy, and went into trousers, and we played Blondin in the glen together."

Still Philip did not speak. He was gripping the stable-wall with his trembling fingers, and struggling for composure. Pete scraped the paving-stones at his feet, and mumbled again in a voice that was near to breaking. "Spake for me, Phil. It's you to do it. You've the way of saying things, and making them out to look something. It would be clane ruined in a jiffy if I did it for myself. Spake for me, boy, now won't you, now?"

Still Philip was silent. He was doing his best to swallow a lump in his throat. His heart had begun to know itself. In the light of Pete's confession he had read his own secret. To give the girl up was one thing; it was another to plead for her for Pete. But Pete's trouble touched him. The lump at his throat went down, and the fingers on the wall slacked away. "I'll do it," he said, only his voice was like a sob.

Then he tried to go off hastily that he might hide the emotion that came over him like a flood that had broken its dam. But Pete gripped him by the shoulder, and peered into his face in the dark. "You will, though," said Pete, with a little shout of joy; "then it's as good as done; God bless you, old fellow."

Philip began to roll about. "Tut, it's nothing," he said, with a stout heart, and then he laughed a laugh with a cry in it. He could have said no more without breaking down; but just then a flash of light fell on them from the house, and a hushed voice cried, "Pete!"

"It's herself," whispered Pete. "She's coming! She's here!"

Philip turned, and saw Kate in the doorway of the dairy, the sweet young figure framed like a silhouette by the light behind.

"I'm going!" said Philip, and he edged up to the house as the girl stepped out.

Pete followed him a step or two in approaching Kate. "Whist, man!" he whispered. "Tell the old geezer I'll be going to chapel reglar early tides and late shifts, and Sunday-school constant. And, whist! tell him I'm larning myself to play on the harmonia."

Then Philip slithered softly through the dairy door, and shut it after him, leaving Kate and Pete together.

VII

The kitchen of "The Manx Fairy" was now savoury with the odour of herrings roasting in their own brine, and musical with the crackling and frizzling of the oil as it dropped into the fire.

"It's a long way back to Ballure, Mrs. Cregeen," said Philip, popping his head in at the door jamb. "May I stay to a bite of supper?"

"Aw, stay and welcome," said Cæsar, putting down the big book, and Nancy Joe said the same, dropping her high-pitched voice perceptibly, and Grannie said, also, "Right welcome, sir, if you'll not be thinking mane to take pot luck with us. Potatoes and herrings, Mr. Christian; just a Manxman's supper. Lift the pot off the slowrie, Nancy."

"Well, and isn't he a Manxman himself, mother?" said Cæsar.

"Of course I am, Mr. Cregeen," said Philip, laughing noisily. "If I'm not, who should be, eh?'"

"And Manxman or no Manxman, what for should he turn up his nose at herrings same as these?" said Nancy Joe. She was dishing up a bowlful. "Where'll he get the like of them? Not in England over, I'll go bail."

"Indeed, no, Nancy," said Philip, still laughing needlessly.

"And if they had them there, the poor, useless creatures would be lost to cook them."

"'Deed, would they, Nancy," said Grannie. She was rolling the potatoes into a heap on to the bare table. "And we've much to be thankful for, with potatoes and herrings three times a day; but we shouldn't be thinking proud of our-selves for that."

"Ask the gentleman to draw up, mother," said Cæsar.

"Draw up, sir, draw up. Here's your bowl of butter-milk. A knife and fork, Nancy. We're no people for knife and fork to a herring, sir. And a plate for Mr. Christian, woman; a gentleman usually likes a plate. Now ate, sir, ate and welcome—but where's your friend, though?"

"Pete! oh! he's not far off." Saying this, Philip interrupted his laughter to distribute sage winks between Nancy Joe and Grannie.

Cæsar looked around with a potato half peeled in his fingers. "And the girl—where's Kate?" he asked.

"She's not far off neither," said Philip, still winking vigorously. "But don't trouble about them, Mr. Cregeen. They'll want no supper. They're feeding on sweeter things than herrings even." Saying this he swallowed a gulp with another laugh.

Cæsar lifted his head with a pinch of his herring between finger and thumb half way to his open mouth. "Were you spaking, sir?" he said.

At that Philip laughed immoderately. It was a relief to drown with laughter the riot going on within.

"Aw, dear, what's agate of the boy?" thought Grannie.

"Is it a dog bite that's working on him?" thought Nancy.

"Speaking!" cried Philip, "of course I'm speaking. I've come in to do it, Mr. Cregeen—I've come in to speak for Pete. He's fond of your daughter, Cæsar, and wants your good-will to marry her."

"Lord-a-massy!" cried Nancy Joe.

"Dear heart alive!" muttered Grannie.

"Peter Quilliam!" said Cæsar, "did you say Peter?"

"I did, Mr. Cregeen, Peter Quilliam," said Philip stoutly, "my friend Pete, a rough fellow, perhaps, and without much education, but the best-hearted lad in the island. Come now, Cæsar, say the word, sir, and make the young people happy."

He almost foundered over that last word, but Cæsar kept him up with a searching look.

"Why, I picked him out of the streets, as you might say," said Cæsar.

"So you did, Mr. Cregeen, so you did. I always thought you were a discerning man, Cæsar. What do you say, Grannie? It's Cæsar for knowing a deserving lad when he sees one, eh?"

He gave another round of his cunning winks, and Grannie replied, "Aw, well, it's nothing against either of them anyway."

Cæsar was gitting as straight as a crowbar and as grim as a gannet. "And when he left me, he gave me imperence and disrespeck."

"But the lad meant no harm, father," said Grannie; "and hadn't you told him to take to the road?"

"Let every bird hatch its own eggs, mother; it'll become you better," said Cæsar. "Yes, sir, the lip of Satan and the imperence of sin."

"Pete!" cried Philip, in a tone of incredulity; "why, he hasn't a thought about you that isn't out of the Prayer-book."

Cæsar snorted. "No? Then maybe that's where he's going for his curses."

"No curses at all," said Nancy Joe, from the side of the table, "but a right good lad though, and you've never had another that's been a patch on him."

Cæsar screwed round to her and said severely, "Where there's geese there's dirt, and where there's women there's talking." Then turning back to Philip, he said in a tone of mock deference, "And may I presume, sir—a little question—being a thing like that's general understood—what's his fortune?"

Philip fell back in his chair. "Fortune? Well, I didn't think that you now——"

"No?" said Cæsar. "We're not children of Israel in the wilderness getting manna dropped from heaven twice a day. If it's only potatoes and herrings itself, we're wanting it three times, you see."

Do what he would to crush it, Philip could not help feeling a sense of relief. Fate was interfering; the girl was not for Pete. For the first moment since he returned to the kitchen he breathed freely and fully. But then came the prick of conscience: he had come to plead for Pete, and he must be loyal; he must not yield; he must exhaust all his resources of argument and persuasion. The wild idea occurred to him to take Cæsar by force of the Bible.

"But think what the old book says, Mr. Cregeen, 'take no thought for the morrow'——"

"That's what Johnny Niplightly said, Mr. Christian, when he lit my kiln overnight and burnt my oats before morning.".

"'But consider the lilies'——"

"I have considered them, sir; but I'm foiling still and mother has to spin."

"And isn't Pete able to toil, too," said Philip boldly. "Nobody better in the island; there's not a lazy bone in his body, and he'll earn his living anywhere."

"What *is* his living, sir?" said Cæsar.

Philip halted for an answer, and then said, "Well, he's only with me in the boat at present, Mr. Cregeen."

"And what's he getting? His meat and drink and a bit of pence, eh? And you'll be selling up some day, it's like, and going away to England over, and then where is he? Let the girl marry a mother-naked man at once."

"But you're wanting help yourself, father," said Grannie. "Yes, you are though, and time for chapel too and aisément in your old days— —"

"Give the lad my mill as well as my daughter, is that it, eh?" said Cæsar. "No, I'm not such a goose as yonder, either. I could get heirs, sir, heirs, bless ye—fifty acres and better, not to spake of the bas'es. But I can do without them. The Lord's blest me with enough. I'm not for daubing grease on the tail of the fat pig."

"Just so, Cæsar," said Philip, "just so; you can afford to take a poor man for your son-in-law, and there's Pete— —"

"I'd be badly in want of a bird, though, to give a groat for an owl," said Cæsar.

"The lad means well, anyway," said Grannie; "and he was that good to his mother, poor thing—it was wonderful."

"I knew the woman," said Cæsar; "I broke a sod of her grave myself. A brand plucked from the burning, but not a straight walker in this life. And what is the lad himself? A monument of sin without a name. A bastard, what else? And that's not the port I'm sailing for."

Down to this point Philip had been torn by conflicting feelings. He was no match for Cæsar in worldly logic, or at fencing with texts of Scripture. The devil had been whispering at his ear, "Let it alone, you'd better." But his time had come at length to conquer both himself and Cæsar. Rising to his feet at Cæsar's last word, he cried in a voice of wrath, "What? You call yourself a Christian man, and punish the child for the sin of the parent! No name, indeed! Let me tell you, Mr. Cæsar Cregeen, it's possible to have one name in heaven that's worse than none at all on earth, and that's the name of a hypocrite."

So saying he threw back his chair, and was making for the door, when Cæsar rose and said softly, "Come into the bar and have something." Then, looking back at Philip's plate, he forced a laugh, and said, "But you've turned over your herring, sir—that's bad luck." And, putting a hand on Philip's shoulder, he added, in a lower tone, "No disrespeck to you, sir; and no harm to the lad, but take my word for it, Mr. Christian, if there's an amble in the mare it'll be in the colt."

Philip went off without another word. The moon was rising and whitening as he stepped from the door. Outside the porch a figure flitted past him in the uncertain shadows with a merry trill of mischievous laughter. He found Pete in the road, puffing and blowing as before, but from a different cause.

"The living devil's in the girl for sartin," said Pete; "I can't get my answer out of her either way." He had been chasing her for his answer, and she had escaped him through a gate. "But what luck with the ould man, Phil?"

Then Phil told him of the failure of his mission—told him plainly and fully but tenderly, softening the hard sayings but revealing the whole truth. As he did so he was conscious that he was not feeling like one who brings bad news. He knew that his mouth in the darkness was screwed up into an ugly smile, and, do what he would; he could not make it straight and sorrowful.

The happy laughter died off Pete's, lips, and he listened at first in silence, and afterwards with low growls. When Phil showed him how his poverty was his calamity he said, "Ay, ay, I'm only a wooden-spoon man." When Phil told him how Cæsar had ripped up their old dead quarrel he muttered, "I'm on the ebby tide, Phil, that's it." And when Phil hinted at what Cæsar had said of his mother and of the impediment of his own birth, a growl came up from the very depths of him, and he scraped the stones under his feet and said, "He shall repent it yet; yes, shall he."

"Come, don't take it so much to heart—it's miserable to bring you such bad news," said Phil; but he knew the sickly smile was on his lips still, and he hated himself for the sound of his own voice.

Pete found no hollow ring in it. "God bless you, Phil," he said; "you've done the best for me, I know that. My pocket's as low as my heart, and it isn't fair to the girl, or I shouldn't be asking the ould man's lave anyway."

He stood a moment in silence, crunching the wooden laths of the garden fence like matchwood in his fingers, and then said, with sudden resolution, "I know what I'll do."

"What's that?" said Philip.. "I'll go abroad; I'll go to Kimberley."

"Never!"

"Yes, will I though, and quick too. You heard what the men were saying in the evening—there's Manx ones going by the boat in the morning? Well, I'll go with them."

"And you talk of being low in your pocket," said Phil. "Why, it will take all you've got, man."

"And more, too," said Pete, "but you'll lend me the lave of the passage-money. That's getting into debt, but no matter. When a man falls into the water he needn't mind the rain. I'll make good money out yonder."

A light had appeared at the window of an upper room, and Pete shook his clenched fist at it and cried, "Good-bye, Master Cregeen. I'll put worlds between us. You were my master once, but nobody made you my master for ever—neither you nor no man."

All this time Philip knew that hell was in his heart. The hand that had let him loose when his anger got the better of him with Cæsar was clutching at him again. Some evil voice at his ear was whispering, "Let him go; lend him the money."

"Come on, Pete," he faltered, "and don't talk nonsense!"

But Pete heard nothing. He had taken a few steps forward, as far as to the stable-yard, and was watching the light in the house. It was moving from window to window of the dark wall. "She's taking the father's candle," he muttered. "She's there," he said softly. "No, she has gone. She's coming back though." He lifted the stocking cap from his head and fumbled it in his hands. "God bless her," he murmured. He sank to his knees on the ground. "And take care of her while I'm away."

The moon had come up in her whiteness behind, and all was quiet and solemn around. Philip fell back and turned away his face.

VIII

When Cæsar came in after seeing Philip to the door, he said, "Not a word of this to the girl. You that are women are like pigs—we've got to pull the way we don't want you."

On that Kate herself came in, blushing a good deal, and fussing about with great vigour. "Are you talking of the piggies, father?" she said artfully. "How tiresome they are, to be sure! They came out into the yard when the moon rose and I had such work to get them back."

Cæsar snorted a little, and gave the signal for bed. "Fairies indeed!" he said, in a tone of vast contempt, going to the corner to wind the clock. "Just wakeness of faith," he said over the clank of the chain as the weights rose; "and no trust in God neither," he added, and then the clock struck ten.

Grannie had lit two candles—one for herself and her husband, the other for Nancy Joe. Nancy had slyly filled three earthenware crocks with water from the well, and had set them on the table, mumbling something about the kettle and the morning. And Cæsar himself, pretending not to see anything, and muttering dark words about waste, went from the clock to the hearth, and raked out the hot ashes to a flat surface, on which you might have laid a girdle for baking cakes.

"Good-night, Nancy," called Grannie, from half-way up the stairs, and Cæsar, with his head down, followed grumbling. Nancy went off next, and then Kate was left alone. She had to put out the lamp and wait for her father's candle.

When the lamp was gone the girl was in the dark, save for the dim light of the smouldering fire. She began to tremble and to laugh in a whisper. Her eyes danced in the red glow of the dying turf. She slipped off her shoes and went to a closet in the wall. There she picked an apple out of a barrel, and brought it to the fire and roasted it. Then, down on her knees before the hearth, she took took two pinches of the apple and swallowed them. After that and a little shudder she rose again, and turned about to go to bed, backwards, slowly, tremblingly, with measured steps, feeling her way past the furniture, having a shock when she touched anything, and laughing to herself, nervously, when she remembered what it was.

At the door of her father's room and Grannie's she called, with a quaver in her voice, and a sleepy grunt came out to her. She reached one hand through the door, which was ajar, and took the burning candle. Then she blew out the light with a trembling puff, that had to be twice repeated, and made for her own bedroom, still going backwards.

It was a sweet little chamber over the dairy, smelling of new milk and ripe apples, and very dainty in dimity and muslin. Two tiny windows looked out from it, one on to the stable-yard and the other on to the orchard. The late moon came through the orchard window, over the heads of the dwarf trees, and the little white place was lit up from the floor to the sloping thatch.

Kate went backwards as far as to the bed, and sat down on it She fancied she heard a step in the yard, but the yard window was at her back, and she would not look behind. She listened, but heard nothing more except a see-sawing noise from the stable, where the mare was running her rope in the manger ring. Nothing but this and the cheep-cheep of a mouse that was gnawing the wood somewhere in the floor.

"Will he come?" she asked herself.

She rose and loosened her gown, and as it fell to her feet she laughed.

"Which will it be, I wonder—which?" she whispered.

The moonlight had crept up to the foot of the bed, and now lay on it like a broad blue sword speckled as with rust by the patchwork counterpane.

She freed her hair from its red ribbon, and it fell in a shower about her face. All around her seemed hushed and awful. She shuddered again, and with a back ward hand drew down the sheets. Then she took a long, deep breath, like a sigh that is half a smile, and lay down to sleep.

IX

Somewhere towards the dawn, in the vague shadow-land between a dream and the awakening, Kate thought she was startled by a handful of rice thrown at her carriage on her marriage morning. The rattle came again, and then she knew it was from gravel dashed at her bedroom window. As she recognised the sound, a voice came as through a cavern, crying, "Kate!" She was fully awake by this time. "Then it's to be Pete," she thought. "It's bound to be Pete, it's like," she told herself. "It's himself outside, anyway."

It was Pete indeed. He was standing in the thin darkness under the window, calling the girl's name out of the back of his throat, and whistling to her in a sort of whisper. Presently he heard a movement inside the room, and he said over his shoulder, "She's coming."

There was the click of a latch and the slithering of a sash, and then out through the little dark frame came a head like a picture, with a face all laughter, crowned by a cataract of streaming black hair, and rounded off at the throat by a shadowy hint of the white frills of a night-dress.

"Kate," said Pete again.

She pretended to have come to the window merely to look out, and, like a true woman, she made a little start at the sound of his voice, and a little cry of dismay at the idea that he was so close beneath and had taken her unawares. Then she peered down into the gloom and said, in a tone of wondrous surprise, "It must be Pete, surely."

"And so it is, Kate," said Pete, "and he couldn't take rest without spaking to you once again."

"Ah!" she said, looking back and covering her eyes, and thinking of Black Tom and the fairies. But suddenly the mischief of her sex came dancing into her blood, and she could not help but plague the lad. "Have you lost your way, Pete?" she asked, with an air of innocence.

"Not my way, but myself, woman," said Pete.

"Lost yourself! Have the lad's wits gone moon-raking, I wonder? Are you witched then, Pete?" she inquired, with vast solemnity.

"Aw, witched enough. Kate——"

"Poor fellow!" sighed Kate. "Did she strike you unknown and sudden?"

"Unknown it was, Kirry, and sudden, too. Listen, though——"

"Aw dear, aw dear! Was it old Mrs. Cowley of the Curragh? Did she turn into a hare? Is it bitten you've been, Pete?"

"Aw, yes, bitten enough. But, Kate——"

"Then it was a dog, it's like. Is it flying from the water you are, Pete?"

"No, but flying *to* the water, woman. Kate, I say——"

"Is it burning they're doing for it?"

"Burning and freezing both. Will you hear me, though? I'm going away—hundreds and thousands of miles away."

Then from the window came a tone of great awe, uttered with face turned upward as if to the last remaining star.

"Poor boy! Poor boy! it's bitten he is, for sure."

"Then it's yourself that's bitten me. Kirry——"

There was a little crow of gaiety. "Me? Am I the witch? You called me a fairy in the road this evening."

"A fairy you are, girl, and a witch too; but listen, now——"

"You said I was an angel, though, at the cowhouse gable; and an angel doesn't bite."

Then she barked like a dog, and laughed a shrill laugh like a witch, and barked again.

But Pete could bear no more. "Go on, then; go on with your capers! Go on!" he cried, in a voice of reproach. "It's not a heart that's at you at all, girl, but only a stone. You see a man going away from the island——"

"From the island?" Kate gasped.

"Middling down in the mouth, too, and plagued out of his life between the ruck of you," continued Pete; "but God forgive you all, you can't help it."

"Did you say you were going out of the island, Pete?"

"Coorse I did; but what's the odds? Africa, Kimberley, the Lord knows where——"

"Kimberley! Not Kimberley, Pete!"

"Kimberley or Timbuctoo, what's it matter to the like of you? A man's coming up in the morning to bid you good-bye before an early sailing, and you're thinking of nothing but your capers and divilments."

"It's you to know what a girl's thinking, isn't it, Mr. Pete? And why are you flying in my face for a word?"

"Flying? I'm not flying. It's driven I am."

"Driven, Pete?"

"Driven away by them that's thinking I'm not fit for you. Well, that's true enough, but they shan't be telling me twice."

"They? Who are they, Pete?"

"What's the odds? Flinging my mother at me, too—poor little mother! And putting the bastard on me, it's like. A respectable man's girl isn't going begging that she need marry a lad without a name."

There was a sudden ejaculation from the window-sash. "Who dared to say that?"

"No matter."

"Whoever they are, you can tell them, if it's me they mean, that, name or no name, when I want to marry I'll marry the man I like."

"If I thought that now, Kitty——"

"As for you, Mr. Pete, that's so ready with your cross words, you can go to your Kimberley. Yes, go, and welcome; and what's more—what's more——"

But the voice of anger, in the half light overhead, broke down suddenly into an inarticulate gurgle.

"Why, what's this?" said Pete in a flurry. "You're not crying though, Kate? Whatever am I saying to you, Kitty, woman? Here, here—bash me on the head for a blockhead and an omathaun."

And Pete was clambering up the wall by the side of the dairy window.

"Get down, then," whispered Kate.

Her wrath was gone in a moment, and Pete, being nearer to her now, could see tears of laughter dancing in her eyes.

"Get down, Pete, or I'll shut the window, I will—yes, I will." And, to show how much she was in earnest in getting out of his reach, she shut up the higher sash and opened the lower one.

"Darling!" cried Pete.

"Hush! What's that?" Kate whispered, and drew back on her knees.

"Is the door of the pig-sty open again?" said Pete.

Kate drew a breath of relief. "It's only somebody snoring," she said.

"The ould man," said Pete. "That's all serene! A good ould sheepdog, that snaps more than, he bites, but he's best when he's sleeping—more safer, anyway."

"What's the good of going away, Pete?" said Kate. "You'd have to make a fortune to satisfy father."

"Others have done it, Kitty—why shouldn't I? Manx ones too—silver kings and diamond kings, and the Lord knows what. No fear of me! When I come back it's a queen you'll be, woman—my queen, anyway, with pigs and cattle and a girl to wash and do for you."

"So that's how you'd bribe a poor girl is it? But you'd have to turn religious, or father would never consent."

"When I come home again, Kitty, I'll be that religious you never seen. I'll be just rolling in it. You'll hear me spaking like the Book of Genesis and Abraham, and his sons, and his cousins; I'll be coming up at night making love to you at the cowhouse door like the Acts of the Apostles."

"Well, that will be some sort of courting, anyway. But who says I'll be wanting it? Who says I'm willing for you to go away at all with the notion that I must be bound to marry you when you come back?"

"I do," said Pete stoutly.

"Oh, indeed, sir."

"Listen. I'll be working like a nigger out yonder, and making my pile, and banking it up, and never seeing nothing but the goold and the girls——"

"My goodness! What do you say?"

"Aw, never fear! I'm a one-woman man, Kate; but loving one is giving me eyes for all. And you'll be waiting for me constant, and never giving a skute of your little eye to them drapers and druggists from Ramsey——"

"Not one of them? Not Jamesie Corrin, even—he's a nice boy, is Jamesie."

"That dandy-divil with the collar? Hould your capers, woman!"

"Nor young Ballawhaine—Ross Christian, you know?"

"Ross Christian be—well, no; but, honour bright, you'll be saying, 'Peter's coming; I must be thrue!'"

"So I've got my orders, sir, eh? It's all settled then, is it? Hadn't you better fix the wedding-day and take out the banns, now that your hand is in? I have got nothing to do with it, seemingly. Nobody asks me."

"Whist, woman!" cried Pete. "Don't you hear it?"

A cuckoo was passing over the house and calling.

"It's over the thatch, Kate. 'Cuckoo! Cuckoo! Cuckoo!' Three times! Bravo! Three times is a good Amen. Omen is it? Have it as you like, love."

The stars had paled out by this time, and the dawn was coming up like a grey vapour from the sea.

"Ugh! the air feels late; I must be going in," said Kate.

"Only a bit of a draught from the mountains—it's not morning yet," said Pete.

A bird called from out of the mist somewhat far away.

"It is, though. That's the throstle up the glen," said Kate.

Another bird answered from the eaves of the house.

"And what's that?" said Pete. "Was it yourself, Kitty? How straight your voice is like the throstle's!"

She hung her head at the sweet praise, but answered tartly, "How people will be talking!"

A dead white light came sweeping over the front of the house, and the trees and the hedges, all quiet until then, began to shudder. Kate shuddered too, and drew the frills closer about her throat. "I'm going, Pete," she whispered.

"Not yet. It's only a taste of the salt from the sea," said Pete. "The moon's not out many minutes."

"Why, you goose, it's been gone these two hours. This isn't Jupiter, where it's moonlight always."

"Always moonlight in Jubiter, is it?" said Pete. "My goodness! What coorting there must be there!"

A cock crowed from under the hen-roost, the dog barked indoors, and the mare began to stamp in her stall.

"When do you sail, Pete?"

"First tide—seven o'clock."

"Time to be off, then. Good-bye!"

"Hould hard—a word first."

"Not a word. I'm going back to bed. See, there's the sun coming up over the mountains."

"Only a touch of red on the tip of ould Cronky's nose. Listen! Just to keep them dandy-divils from plaguing you, I'll tell Phil to have an eye on you while I'm away."

"Mr. Christian?"

"Call him Philip, Kate. He's as free as free. No pride at all. Let him take care of you till I come back."

"I'm shutting the window, Pete!"

"Wait! Something else. Bend down so the ould man won't hear."

"I can't reach—what is it?"

"Your hand, then; I'll tell it to your hand."

She hesitated a moment, and then dropped her hand over the window-sill, and he clutched at it and kissed it, and pushed back the white sleeve and ran up the arm with his lips as far as he could climb.

"Another, my girl; take your time, one more—half a one, then."

She drew her arm back until her hand got up to his hand, and then she said, "What's this? The mole on your finger still, Pete? You called me a witch—now see me charm it away. Listen!—'Ping, ping, prash, Cur yn cadley-jiargan ass my chass.'"

She was uttering the Manx charm in a mock-solemn ululation when a bough snapped in the orchard, and she cried, "What's that?"

"It's Philip. He's waiting under the apple-tree," said Pete.

"My goodness me!" said Kate, and down went the window-sash.

A moment later it rose again, and there was the beautiful young face in its frame as before, but with the rosy light of the dawn on it.

"Has he been there all the while?" she whispered.

"What matter? It's only Phil."

"Good-bye! Good luck!" and then the window went down for good.

"Time to go," said Philip, still in his tall silk hat and his knickerbockers. He had been standing alone among the dead brown fern, the withering gorse, and the hanging brambles, gripping the apple-tree and swallowing the cry that was bubbling up to his throat, but forcing himself to look upon Pete's happiness, which was his own calamity, though it was tearing his heart out, and he could hardly bear it.

The birds were singing by this time, and Pete, going back, sang and whistled with the best of them.

X

In the mists of morning, Grannie had awakened in her bed with the turfy scraas of the thatch just visible above her, and the window-blind like a hazy moon floating on the wall at her side. And, fixing her nightcap, she had sighed and said, "I can't close my eyes for dreaming that the poor lad has come to his end untimeously."

Cæsar yawned, and asked, "What lad?"

"Young Pete, of course," said Grannie.

Cæsar *umpht* and grunted.

"We were poor ourselves when we began, father."

Grannie felt the glare of the old man's eye on her in the darkness. "'Deed, we were; but people forget things. We had to borrow to buy our big overshot wheel; we had, though. And when ould Parson Harrison sent us the first boll of oats, we couldn't grind it for want of——"

Cæsar tugged at the counterpane and said, "Will you lie quiet, woman, and let a hard-working man sleep?"

"Then don't be the young man's destruction, Cæsar."

Cæsar made a contemptuous snort, and pulled the bedclothes about his head.

"Aw, 'deed, father, but the girl might do worse. A fine, strapping lad. And, dear heart, the cheerful face *at* him! It's taking joy to look at—like drawing water from a well! And the laugh *at* the boy, too—that joyful, it's as good to hear in the morning as six pigs at a lit——"

"Then marry the lad yourself, woman, and have done with it," cried Cæsar, and, so saying, he kicked out his leg, turned over to the wall, and began to snore with great vigour.

XI

The tide was up in Ramsey Harbour, and rolling heavily on the shore before a fresh sea-breeze with a cold taste of the salt in it. A steamer lying by the quay was getting up steam; trucks were running on her gangways, the clanking crane over her hold was working, and there was much shouting of name, and ordering and protesting, and general tumult. On the after-deck stood the emigrants for Kimberley, the Quarks from Glen Rushen, and some of the young Gills from Castletown—stalwart lads, bearing themselves bravely in the midst of a circle of their friends, who talked and laughed to make them forget they were on the point of going.

Pete and Phil came up the quay, and were received by a shout of incredulity from Quayle, the harbour-master. "What, are you going, too, Mr. Philip?" Philip answered him "No," and passed on to the ship.

Pete was still in his stocking cap and Wellington boots, but he had a monkey-jacket over his blue guernsey. Except for a parcel in a red print handkerchief, this was all his kit and luggage. He felt a little lost amid all the bustle, and looked helpless and unhappy. The busy preparations on land and shipboard had another effect on Philip. He sniffed the breeze off the bay and laughed, and said, "The sea's calling me, Pete; I've half a mind to go with you."

Pete answered with a watery smile. His high spirits were failing him at last. Five years were a long time to be away, if one built all one's hopes on coming back. So many things might happen, so many chances might befall. Pete had no heart for laughter.

Philip had small mind for it, either, after the first rush of the salt in his blood was over. He felt at some moments as if hell itself were inside of him. What troubled him most was that he could not, for the life of him, be sorry that Pete was leaving the island. Once or twice since they left Sulby he had been startled by the thought that he hated Pete. He knew that his lip curled down hard at sight of Pete's solemn face. But Pete never suspected this, and the innocent tenderness of the rough fellow was every moment beating it down with blows that cut like ice and burnt like fire.

They were standing by the forecastle head, and talking above the loud throbbing of the funnel.

"Good-bye, Phil; you've been wonderful good to me—better nor anybody in the world. I've not been much of a chum for the like of you, either—you that's college bred and ought to be the first gentry in the island if everybody had his own. But you shan't be ashamed for me, neither—no you shan't, so help me God! I won't be long away, Phil—maybe five years, maybe less, and when I come back you'll be the first Manxman living. No? But you will, though; you will, I'm telling you. No nonsense at all, man. Lave it to me to know."

Philip's frosty blue eyes began to melt.

"And if I come back rich, I'll be your ould friend again as much as a common man may; and if I come back poor and disappointed and done for, I'll not claim you to disgrace you; and if I never come back at all, I'll be saying to myself in my dark hour somewhere, 'He'll spake up for you at home, boy; *he'll* not forget you.'"

Philip could hear no more for the puffing of the steam and the clanking of the chains.

"Chut! the talk a man will put out when he's thinking of ould times gone by!"

The first bell rang on the bridge, and the harbour-master shouted, "All ashore, there!"

"Phil, there's one turn more I'll ask of you, and, if it's the last, it's the biggest."

"What is it?"

"There's Kate, you know. Keep an eye on the girl while I'm away. Take a slieu round now and then, and put a sight on her. She'll not give a skute at the heirs the ould man's telling of; but them young drapers and druggists, they'll plague the life out of the girl. Bate them off, Phil. They're not worth a fudge with their fists. But don't use no violence. Just duck the dandy-divils in the harbour—that'll do."

"No harm shall come to her while you are away."

"Swear to it, Phil. Your word's your bond, I know that; but give me your hand and swear to it—it'll be more surer."

Philip gave his hand and his oath, and then tried to turn away, for he knew that his face was reddening.

"Wait! There's another while your hand's in, Phil. Swear that nothing and nobody shall ever come between us two."

"You know nothing ever will."

"But swear to it, Phil. There's bad tongues going, and it'll make me more aisier. Whatever they do, whatever they say, friends and brothers to the last?"

Philip felt a buzzing in his head, and he was so dizzy that he could hardly stand, but he took the second oath also. Then the bell rang again, and there was a great hubbub. Gangways were drawn up, ropes were let go, the captain called to the shore from the bridge, and the blustering harbour-master called to the bridge from the shore.

"Go and stand on the end of the pier, Phil—just aback of the lighthouse—and I'll put myself at the stern. I want a friend's face to be the last thing I see when I'm going away from the old home."?

Philip could bear no more. The hate in his heart was mastered. It was under his feet. His flushed face was wet.

The throbbing of the funnels ceased, and all that could be heard was the running of the tide in the harbour and the wash of the waves on the shore. Across the sea the sun came up boldly, "like a guest expected," and down its dancing water-path the steamer moved away. Over the land old Bar-rule rose up like a sea king with hoar-frost on his forehead, and the smoke began to lift from the chimneys of the town at his feet.

"Good-bye, little island, good-bye! I'll not forget you. I'm getting kicked out of you, but you've been a good ould mother to me, and, God help me, I'll come back to you yet. So long, little Mona, s'long? I'm laving you, but I'm a Manxman still."

Pete had meant to take off his stocking cap as they passed the lighthouse, and to dash the tears from his eyes like a man. But all that Philip could see from the end of the pier was a figure huddled up at the stern on a coil of rope.